Presenting
LADY GUS

Presenting LADY GUS

A Georgian-Era Romance

Second Edition

Sydney Jane Baily

Cat Whisker Press

Massachusetts

Published by Cat Whisker Press

Cover: Philip Ré
Book Design: Cat Whisker Studio
Editor: Chloe Bearuski

ISBN: 9781957421414
Second Edition, 2024

DEDICATION

To Jasper
My creative, curious, comical son
Whose uniqueness I wholeheartedly admire.

I love you to the moon and much, much farther!

ACKNOWLEDGMENTS

Sincere thanks to my fellow authors at Love Historicals for their encouragement: Christy Carlyle, Gina Danna, Jill Hughey, Catherine Kean, Anna Markland, Nancy Morse, Laurel O'Donnell, Margery Scott, and Cynthia Woolf.

A special thanks to my cover designer, Philip Ré, who patiently made small change after small change until Lady Gus and her Captain look positively perfect.

CHAPTER ONE

1806, Thornbury Castle, Gloucestershire, England

"Augusta," the elder Brenville's voice carried ahead of him as he dashed along the brightly lit corridor toward the solar that once belonged to King Henry VIII. As he neared, Jerome Brenville yelled his daughter's name once more—gleefully, joyfully—for today he had placed a seal on all their bright tomorrows, which till recently had looked very dim indeed. His deceased wife was surely smiling down at him. His daughter would be pleased as well.

And he loved to please her. The very sight of her face, tanned from too many hours spent walking and gardening, and her sweet smile, and her bright eyes were as dear to him as all the gold in King George's coffers.

He heard her familiar whistling, just before he burst into the room.

AUGUSTA CLOSED HER LIPS, swallowing the last notes, and rose from the table. She had labored long all that morning with the accounts and the ancient abacus to extend their meager revenue to pay all the servants of their vast estate, which her father had dutifully inherited and stoically, stubbornly, refused to give up.

Putting a hand to her temple that throbbed slightly, she rang the bell for tea. Yes, tea would put absolutely everything right—except she had come up with the sad truth that however much she pared down the manor's expenses, she could not pay for what they needed while putting money aside for the king's taxes. She simply had not enough coinage to keep them in food and wine, or even watery ale, for another six months.

She rubbed her neck and bent over nearly double to stretch her long frame. Up again, deep breath, then down, as she stretched.

Lord Brenville bent down, too, then up, then down along with her, trying to look her in the eye. "Cease this infernal motion, daughter. I have great news."

"What is it, Father?" Knowing him, he might have agreed to purchase a coal mine in the middle of the Indian Ocean or fishing rights in the Welsh foothills. For Jerome Brenville, last male in a line that stretched back to before the Norman invasion, let money slip through his fingers like water from the pump, and he had done so with a considerable fortune over his long lifetime.

"I have *found* him."

"Him?" Augusta prompted, rubbing a hand to the small of her back.

"Your husband!" he said, with not the smallest note of triumph.

She blanched. Her father had finally snapped under the pressure of their dwindling resources.

"Father," she spoke slowly, "I don't have a husband."

"No, no, Augusta, keep up, please. I have found your *future* husband. At long last. None too soon, may I add. He will save us all."

"Save us!" That galled her though she had to admit she was as eager to have a husband as her father was to have her wed to one. Not to mention the dreaded deadline of her grandfather's will being nearly upon them.

She walked hurriedly around the table between them, until she tripped over the hound who was always directly at her feet or wending its way through her skirts. She landed on top of the dog who took it as kindly as he had every other trip and fall. She stayed where she was, absently rubbing the dog's large belly with her hand.

As she looked up at her father with his kind brown eyes and puckish mouth, she wanted to ask a hundred questions at once, yet only one came out.

"Has this man agreed?"

"Yes, yes. The name of Brenville still means something in this realm. He signed the agreement I put forth. I just signed it myself, sealed it, and sent it back to him. He could be here within a month, a fortnight if he hurries."

"Have I ever met him?" she asked, wondering how she could be speaking so calmly. She really wanted to ask if he were young and handsome or old and decrepit? Would he be kind or cruel? Most important perhaps, would she be able to tolerate him bedding her? Perhaps, God willing, she would bear his babes if he were still virile. Was he? But these were not things one discussed with one's father.

"No, you've never met. He is from the far east."

Shocked, she jumped to her feet, spilling the dog onto its other side. "A heathen! An infidel!" she exclaimed. "From . . . from Nepal or . . . Persia ?" What had her father done? Even her dog growled at the tenseness in her voice.

"No, no, dear. From Kent, Ramsgate actually," Lord Brenville reassured her.

"Phew," she said, letting go a long sigh of relief. Kent, the eastern most county of England, as far east as her

estate was to the west. Her breath caught in her throat. Her own dear, dear Thornbury, within easy distance of the bustling city of Bristol and the restorative waters of Bath. How she loved it here.

"Will I have to live in Ramsgate?" she asked. "For I don't think they do much there except grow hops and shuck oysters, Father. I'm not sure if I could—"

Jerome Brenville touched his daughter's cheek, too bronzed, she knew, to ever be called fair. And she stopped speaking to smile at him.

"Your place is here, your life is here. I have told your future husband this, and he has agreed."

She smiled and took his hand, squeezing it with all the gratitude she felt. He had ever been a lenient and tolerant father, and she had tried to repay his trust in her by being the best steward of his estate, the kind she knew her mother would have been had she lived.

"How did you meet him?"

"He is the friend of the youngest son of a dear friend of my cousin Walter. You remember Walter Montmorency, from Sittingbourne, though he was raised not a hairsbreadth from Chipping Norton. We became quite close when we were at Oxford—"

"Father," she interrupted.

"I know, I know what you're going to say."

Augusta waited.

"Chipping Norton proper is vastly different from the outskirts—"

"Father, who cares about blasted Chipping Norton. I want to know if you know this man, my future husband, or not?"

After all, they'd had a few missteps on the path to her getting married, including three untimely deaths of potentially decent husbands and a number of god-awful, entirely inappropriate suitors.

"Well," he dragged the word out as long as he could. "In absolute truth, I have never laid eyes upon him. However," he rushed on as she sat back down with a thud, the chair nearly slipping out from under her, "by all accounts, he is sound of mind and body. A captain in the King's navy, a youngest son who has amassed his own wealth by the sweat of his brow, if not the brains in his head."

All useful information, Augusta allowed, but more than that, she wanted to know his height and his temperament. Yet her father could not know, as he had never seen him.

"I know that he early captured Admiral Sir John Jervis's notice and the price of his commission was waived. He served under Commodore Nelson, and from all accounts, he has been indispensable in certain foreign endeavors."

"A spy?" she asked.

Her father shrugged. "Who knows, who cares? I am told he has retired, at least for now, with the King's blessing and craves home and hearth, a wife and land of his own. And that's where you and the Brenville estates come in."

"And he doesn't mind being so far from his own home?"

Again her father shrugged. "As the youngest, there was probably nothing offered him by way of land. More, I do not know. I only know that when cousin Walter met the captain, he thought of you, offered on your behalf, and that the young man has agreed. You know Walter and I have been looking for well over a year."

More like four, she thought sourly.

"We need to get you married off. And promptly," Jerome Brenville continued. Our options are limited, given the . . .," he coughed and looked ashamed, "the *small* matter of our debt."

"Which is not so small, Father."

"Exactly, exactly, and since we have not the wealth to entice many a marriageable man of good breeding, how fortunate that we have found one who brings his own wealth. And you are not—"

"I know, I know. I am not the dewy young maiden many a man would desire."

"Bite your tongue," her father admonished. "I was going to say you are not the simpering, empty-headed female many men covet. You are smart and practical and . . ."

She frowned as her father trailed off. Even her own father couldn't praise her with any of the more womanly attributes of her sex. "And he has agreed sight unseen, caring not what I look like?"

"What is wrong with how you look, my daughter?"

She didn't want to consider the litany of her less than exquisite features, starting with her plain brown hair. Instead, she shrugged.

"It merely seems to me as if a wealthy man in the King's favor could—"

"Could hardly do better than you, dear Augusta. After all, young landed ladies are not so easy to come by."

Give or take a few of her own shortcomings, she knew her father was correct. If this man from Kent really wanted land, he could hardly do better than that which surrounded Thornbury castle. Indeed, she and her father would be living a gentile existence with the land's many merits, not to mention the rents, if not for her father's poor judgment in a few painfully expensive and ill-conceived dealings that had gone horribly awry.

This man, this alliance, was their chance to get back on solid ground. This was *her* chance not to be the old maid she had feared she would become as one year slipped so swiftly into the next. And, of course, without a husband, she could hardly meet her grandfather's terms of inheritance. She must marry and beget an heir by her twenty-fifth birthday or the castle would go to the next male Brenville.

She swore a silent oath at the thought of him causing so much worry and angst even from the grave.

"Forget *my* virtues, Father," she said, "tell me more of my future husband. What is his name, pray tell?"

"Rolf," her father said succinctly. The dog wagged its tail against the threadbare oriental carpet.

"Rolf," she repeated. The dog lifted its shaggy head.

"Of Kent," her father added, smiling at her once more.

"Rolf," she echoed as the dog stood up. "But, Father, Rolf is . . ."

"I know, strange coincidence, is it not, that your hound and your husband should share a name?"

She leant against the edge of the desk and recited, "Augusta Elizabeth Jerome Brenville of Thornbury to marry Rolf."

"Of Kent," her father reminded her.

"Of Kent," she amended.

"Woof," barked Rolf.

CHAPTER TWO

"They're coming," Millie shrieked, startling Augusta and practically deafening her a moment after bursting into her private parlor without any type of by-your-leave.

"Millicent, please," Augusta admonished her maid, as she bent to pick up the petit point that she had flung into the air with fright. "You must compose yourself."

"Good Lord," Augusta muttered to herself. Her nerves were frayed enough as it was, without Millie screeching as if the French army were attacking. Her heart was now pounding like a smithy's iron.

"I assume you are trying to tell me that my betrothed is approaching," Augusta said, setting the needlepoint aside and arising from the chair that she'd been frozen in for the better part of the week. There had been times over the past four years when she thought she would glide up the aisle of their dear St. Mary's with flowers in her hair and a fiancé awaiting, only to end up accompanying a casket to the altar.

She walked on trembling legs to the window, having already heard the herald's horn that indicated someone approached.

"That's what I said, milady." Millie was utterly undaunted by her mistress's reproach. "Riders coming up fast from the east."

By this time, Augusta was leaning out the casement to see for herself. She'd always loved this room, cozy of size with windows overlooking the main entrance to one side and the courtyard to the other. Millie was exactly correct, of course. There were indeed men on horseback. On powerful war horses, not the gentle mares she was used to, nor the ungainly workhorses that pulled their plows.

These were horses that looked as if they meant business, as did the men who rode them. Young men, perhaps, . . . maybe handsome men. Her husband was one of the two.

She actually shivered and leaned out a little farther until, somehow, her feet lost contact with the polished floor and her hips seemed to be clearing the sage-green painted sill of the tall window.

Before she could even register that she was about to plunge to her death, and before she could let loose the scream that bubbled up inside her, Augusta felt herself tugged firmly back into her bedroom.

"Shall we go downstairs and greet them, milady?" Millie asked with her usual knack for quietly solving young Lady Brenville's penchant for dire situations. At the same time, she smoothed her mistress's skirts before heading for the door.

"Yes," Augusta agreed, still feeling her heart racing in her chest.

However, instead of following Millie to the hallway, she picked up the small mirror from her bureau. She hadn't known exactly what day Rolf of Kent would arrive, but she had taken extra pains with her appearance almost since her father had told her of his impending arrival. It was her duty to give her soon-to-be-husband a good first impression or, at least, the best that she could muster.

Was she indeed presenting a pleasing semblance?

Her reflection looked quizzically back at her. Her hair was tied up in a fancy style that Millie had been practicing on her all week. Her dress was a flattering shade of indigo, if a trifle old as it was her mother's. And her skin was clear of any pox or rash, though it was still tawny despite staying indoors for the better part of the last two weeks.

"You look fine, milady. Truly," Millie assured her, waiting by the door.

Augusta sighed and turned her eyes to her astonishingly beautiful maid. It was so easy for Millicent Collicott to look like a princess, even in hand-me-down clothes and a white cap upon her head of thick blond hair. Still, she smiled gratefully at her maid's loyalty.

"Let us go down and meet them, then." Augusta hoped she sounded steadier than she felt. "Rolf, come." Her ever-present hound was at her heels instantly.

For years, Augusta had hoped to marry, having passed a suitable decent marriageable age four birthdays hence. Unfortunately, suitors had been few due to her father's inability to provide even the smallest of dowries and the few there had been . . .

How fervently Augusta hoped Rolf of Kent would not be feeble minded, nor cruel natured, nor too disagreeable of face. Moreover, she most hoped that he was not desirous only of the warm, yellow stone that made up her lovely home.

Indeed, the last suitor had literally wanted each and every stone of their historic Tudor residence to build his own house in the north. What's more, he'd seemed almost perturbed that he would have to take her along, though he allowed that he would do so since she would be his wife. She had sent him packing with the haste he deserved.

Augusta had encountered all such men and was still amazed that someone as undiscerning and even indiscriminate as herself had had such a difficult time finding a husband. After all, she was no maverick, holding out for love or convent. She simply wanted a decent man and children, and to remain in her home and to do her father proud.

To that end, she'd prayed on her knees all week that Rolf of Kent was the answer, for she was getting too long in the tooth to be anyone's blushing bride, not to mention being exceedingly curious about the marriage bed. Even Millie had already enjoyed those pleasures though not within the bonds of holy matrimony.

Augusta almost envied Millie's station. As a lady's maid, she had so much more freedom. True, she was a good servant, at times even a friendly ear with whom to chat, but Millie also had a beau who brought her flowers from Augusta's own gardens and gave her ribbons when he could afford them to adorn Millie's lovely blond locks. And, if she could be believed, Millie had allowed Jared many liberties of a late evening in the servants quarters. And when money permitted, Jared had promised to take her as his wife.

Augusta smiled sourly at her own thoughts. It was always about money, it seemed—particularly not having it!

"Come, come, milady," Millie urged her to a quicker pace as they descended the side stairs, the quickest way to the main entrance through which Rolf was sure to come. Jerome Brenville had thought it best that he see the great hall first, though Augusta worried over its cavernous emptiness, sadly bereft of furnishings. Some had fallen apart, some she had been forced to sell.

Augusta followed closely behind her maid, whistling softly in time to the sound of their footfalls on the stone steps, along with Rolf's clattering toenails as he ran in front of them both.

Suddenly, her foot caught in the hem of her gown and she tripped.

Millie, used to her lady's ways, stopped dead and thrust her arms out to brace herself against both sides of the narrow stone stairwell just as Augusta thumped into her from behind.

"Thank you, Millie," Augusta said as they both straightened their gowns. "Is my hair alright?"

"Fine, milady." She tucked in a stray lock of her mistress's hair.

Augusta took a deep breath, and they went along the corridor and out the main doorway whose doors stood open wide. Her father was already outside as were most of the staff, looking upon Rolf of Kent as their blessed savior.

ROLF WAS STILL ASTRIDE his horse when the household began to spill out of the great double doors. Yet he had trouble tearing his gaze from the gorgeous edifice that had become even lovelier as he'd ridden closer. A creamy-colored stone curtain spread out symmetrically, with a central gatehouse and octagonal corner towers, among other smaller structures, crenellations across the top of everything, and a hundred windows winking in the sun.

It was a magnificent home, with the styling of a castle but without the foreboding of an actual stronghold. Soon, as husband to Lady Augusta, it would be his home, too.

Finally, he glanced at the amassing people, searching first for Augusta Brenville, hoping she was passing fair, though frankly, the estate would make up for a few warts and a case of the gout if she be so afflicted. He assumed her father, Lord Brenville, was the older man in fine clothes, who moved forward with a butler in tow, but he saw no sign of his bride, only a throng of servants.

His companion in battle and dearest friend, Peregrine, dismounted first, handing his reins to the waiting stableboy. Before Rolf could do the same, two more figures emerged, one of them no doubt his bride. He was certain of it.

A broad grin broke over his face. Glancing at Perry, he received a congratulatory smile. She was comely indeed, as well as buxom. She was slender, she was pale, she was flaxen-haired. She was . . . a lady's maid.

Belatedly he realized by the manor of her garb that the breathtaking female in question could not be the daughter of the house. Then he noticed the woman who followed.

Rolf's smile did not die on his face. It merely froze slightly. Surely, this was Augusta. She was not beautiful, yet nor was she ugly.

He was about to take stock of her physical qualities, thinking only that there was nothing outstanding about her, when she disappeared—simply disappeared from his view.

Sweet Jesus! Apparently, she'd tripped.

Dismounting quickly, he felt it was his duty to aid her, but her father and her maid were already helping her up by the time he made his way through the servants.

She was blushing as he approached, with a rosy glow on skin that was already nut-colored from the sun. So this was his fair bride.

"My lady, are you well?"

"Yes, I simply made a misstep."

Indeed, he thought, she appeared none the worse for wear as she looked up at him with an earnest coppery-brown gaze. Yes, he quite liked her eyes. Frank, intelligent, discerning. As for her crowning glory, her hair was neither light nor dark, merely a medium shade of brown, rather like his horse's mane and tail. It was wound in so many coils, though, that she looked rather snaky.

To his amazement, three of the coils sprang free as he stared, probably due to her fall. He dodged back as they leapt out at him before settling around her shoulders, long and thick, which he liked.

And then he looked at her mouth, as she muttered, "Oh dear!" And he thought it a pretty mouth, not the fullest of lips, but softly pink and sweetly curved.

"Oh, milady," exclaimed her maid, and Rolf turned his gaze to her once more, and felt the smallest pang of regret. This girl was every man's dream, right down to her sky-blue eyes and puckish lips, the lower one slightly fuller, begging a man to nibble it.

AUGUSTA SIGHED. SO MUCH for first impressions. She knew she looked ridiculous now and momentarily considered whether to pull the rest of her pins out and wear her hair all unfashionably down or try to put the three errant locks back up?

Before she could make more of a mess, Millie had pinned her curls to resemble the rest of her hairstyle. To top it off, Augusta's knees stung terribly where they had come in crushing contact with the stone walkway. At least her future husband now knew what to expect in the way of beauty and grace.

Her husband! She raised her eyes to him. He was tall, as a royal army officer should be. He was young, too, perhaps in his late twenties or early thirties.

"Praise be," she muttered, continuing her appraisal.

He was not ugly, nor did he look cruel. He was, however, dirty—extremely so. His hair, which hung long around his neck, was coated with dust from the journey and his face was smeared with grime, as were his worn clothes. Not at all what she'd hoped from a wealthy suitor.

Why had he not bathed at an inn the night before or at least stopped to wash in one of the many streams round about the area? For certainly, by the look of his wet pants, he had crossed a few on horseback. At the very least, he could have spat on a cloth and wiped his face.

Still, she smiled as he took her hand. She looked down to see how her hand looked in his and was shocked to see black under his fingernails. She swallowed and looked up at his face. It was pleasant, even handsome under the grime, she reminded herself. She heard Rolf clear his throat.

"Lady Brenville, reports of your beauty and charm do not do you justice."

She couldn't stifle the laugh. It broke from her, and she nearly choked. Poor man, what a thing to say, clearly rehearsed and so demonstrably wrong. As if anyone had ever reported anything of her beauty and charm. She laughed until tears came to her eyes. He was nervous, too, she realized. What a relief.

Rolf looked disconcertedly toward her father, who merely shrugged, hardly helping with his round face in a false smile. Finally, it appeared that Rolf understood he had not offended her, and he smiled too.

Augusta's laughter died instantly. *By Jove's arse!* She couldn't help but stare at the dark hole where a tooth should be. At least it was not right in the front of his mouth. Some might view the gap on the left of his smile as quite dashing. And most likely, she consoled herself, he could whistle well.

At last, she managed to reply, "Then you have the advantage, my lord, for I know very little of you, except that you have fought overseas and have served our king well."

He took in her praise like a cat licking cream. So he was a creature of pride as most men. Indeed, his chest seemed to swell even larger than its already generous size.

"I have done my duty," he admitted, and she was impressed by his attempt to sound humble. "Please, call me Rolf," he added.

Her dog, sitting close beside her, barked once.

She hesitated at the rush to intimacy that using first names implied, but if he wished it, then she could be gracious and do the same.

"Yes, of course. And you may call me Augusta. Won't you and your . . .?" she trailed off as she looked past Rolf to see another equally grimy individual, about the same age as her future husband, certainly identical in naval uniforms and in cleanliness, or lack thereof.

"This is Lieutenant Peregrine Newbury, my dearest friend."

"Lady Brenville," the man said, offering her a brief bow. "And please call me Perry as does everyone who knows me."

She offered him a nod. "You are welcome here," she told him. "We have an excellent repast awaiting you both. But perhaps you would care to retire to your rooms first and wash away the remains of your journey?"

Not to mention your previous night's meal, if that were indeed a trail of greasy capon on her betrothed's lapel, as she suspected.

Augusta most definitely didn't want to think of these men sitting upon her furniture or dining at her table, not in their present condition!

But to her dismay, the two companions merely looked at each other in wonder. Then Rolf gave his wide-gapped grin again. Rather charming actually, she decided.

"That is not necessary. Indeed, we are wretchedly hungry. Too hungry for the ceremony of a bath. In any case, we are used to dining aboard our ship or on the battlefield. We have no need of washing."

"Indeed," she muttered, turning to lead the way. Well, if her groom ever hoped to bed her, he'd better find a need for washing—and soon.

THEY GOT THROUGH THE meal but barely. Augusta couldn't help cringing every time Rolf or his friend touched anything. The conversation, however, was perfectly acceptable. Rolf and Perry asked about the land, the nearby villages, the town, the river, even the marketplace, almost as if they were gathering intelligence for a military campaign. Augusta felt nothing but pride and pleasure as she or her father answered their myriad questions. But later in her bedroom, she could recall only her future husband's fingernails.

"What *is* the man thinking?" she railed to Millie as her maid assisted her out of layer upon layer of clothing. "To dine at our table on the first night, filthy like that! How shall I ever bear his presence?"

"Mayhap he was as he stated so plainly, milady, merely too tired after the journey. I'm sure tomorrow both gentlemen can be persuaded to take baths."

"Perhaps you are right." Augusta tugged so hard at her chemise that she ripped it.

"Damnation," she swore. "I think my affliction has worsened since first I heard that I was to be wed." She let Millie exchange her nightdress for another.

"Just your nerves, milady. My sister could give you something that would ease them."

Augusta was well aware of Millie's sister's reputation for healing and midwifery, and had even called on her a few times to help with minor ailments among her household staff.

However, the last thing she wanted right then was a calming potion in case it made her drowsy. She wanted to be as alert and aware as possible, in case of any of her self-inflicted mishaps. Besides, if Millie were right about the men's cleanliness improving, then she would feel better about the impending nuptials.

The next day, however, had proved her maid wrong. For not only did captain and lieutenant not request hot baths, they actually became dirtier after a long ride around the estates.

Rolf was taking stock of all that would be his, Augusta realized, though that day, he had spared hardly a moment to get to know her, the person with whom he would spend the rest of his life.

By evening, when Rolf attempted to engage her in conversation, she'd been so annoyed by his long absence and his greasy hair, she'd withdrawn early. The following day was no better.

"Augusta, I like him," her father had said emphatically when they'd closeted themselves in the king's solar, as they fondly called it. "He is not a stupid man. I've spent many an hour conversing with him these past two days. He already has plans for improving the manor."

"Plans! What plans?" Augusta was not in the mood to hear that Rolf of Kent with his dirty hands was making plans for her lovely home.

"What's more," her father added with glee, "he has the money to do it. He is just the man we need."

"Perhaps," was all she could muster. Maybe she should tell her father that she could never go to bed with such a man. That she could never love such a man.

"Augusta, aren't you happy with your future husband?" Jerome Brenville had come close to put an arm around his daughter's shoulders.

She looked at her father then, a deep frown etched in his forehead, and he suddenly seemed old to her for the first time in her life. And she knew that precisely when he should be relaxing, with the burden of their financial problems nearly solved, she was putting that look of worry onto his kind face. Whatever her problems with Rolf, she would handle them herself.

"Yes, yes of course, Father. I'm only nervous about all the change. I'll be fine when I get used to . . . to Rolf of Kent and to sharing Thornbury with him."

Her father's face broke into a smile, and he seemed years younger. "That's my girl. If it weren't for you, there wouldn't be a castle left to share with him. I've just had a good thought: Tomorrow, I'm going to send out the announcements to the vicar and we'll start working on the invitations to the guests at the same time. I'm so proud of you," he added, before kissing her cheek and heading off to bed.

Little did he know that she'd already written the invitations in the time she'd spent waiting for her grubby bridegroom.

For a moment, she stared into the fire, brightly dancing in the stone hearth. Rolf was planning to go into the town with her father the following morning. She rarely rode due to her tendency to lean too far one way or the other and fall off, even when riding sidesaddle. When she was younger, her parents feared she would break a bone or worse, and thus, she'd been carriage-bound ever since.

Would Rolf deign to forego his exquisite horse to drive in a carriage with her to meet the local folk? Recalling the state of him, Augusta shuddered to think of the impression he would make on the people who had known her all her life and who would be curious to see what kind of match she had finally made. If only he would bathe!

At once, she had decided not to go. Instead, the next morning, she'd wandered idly about Thornbury, wishing she had simply had the nerve to ask her future husband for the money to start replenishing the food stores and paying the servants. When there was no partridge, pigeon, or duck, very little bread, and no pudding at the evening meal, he would no doubt understand the dire situation and contribute to the castle coffers.

By afternoon, hopelessly distracted, she went for a walk to the close-by stream, her dog by her side. Here was a place that she always loved to sit and dream and think and hope. Here was where secretly she'd wished for a good husband and sweet babes.

To the stream she now came, thinking of the impossibility of telling her father it would not work out with the captain. Rolf was comely enough, she supposed, certainly young enough, strong enough. But he seemed to be only a naval officer and nothing more.

Whistling and absently stroking Rolf who lay by her side, Augusta could not get past the captain's dirty face and hands, never mind the fact that they had made no initial connection of mind or spirit.

As if she'd conjured him, suddenly, there he was and without Peregrine. As she looked up at the sound of footsteps, he was already merely a few yards away. Scrambling awkwardly to her feet, she realized that this was the first time they'd been alone since he'd arrived. And it seemed, too, that he looked a bit less grubby.

Rolf crossed his arms and leant against an alder tree. "It seems, Lady Brenville, that I do not suit."

Stunned, she thought he had read her mind.

He continued, "Miss Millicent has made me the offer of a bath so many times in the past two days that I am starting to think she longs to see me unclothed. But perhaps there is another reason. Has her mistress expressed displeasure in her future husband?"

Augusta shrugged. Best to tell him outright, she decided. "I am not used to a seaman's appearance. I suppose I could wish you a tad cleaner, sir."

"And you see that I am." He pushed away from the tree and spread his arms wide as if offering himself for her perusal.

His face held no traces of dirt, but his hair still looked less than clean. His clothes too, were still grimy. But she was pleased to be able to see the complexion of his skin.

"Yes," she agreed. "You do seem less . . . filthy."

He laughed. "Millicent left yet another bowl of lemons and warm water in my room. I decided to take the hint."

Augusta smiled. She had no idea her maid had been working so hard on her behalf. He hadn't bathed, but it was a start.

"Now, at least I can see your face, Rolf."

The dog stood and leaned against her leg.

"What do you think, now that you can see it?" He moved a few feet closer.

Augusta felt her face grow warm. Yet after all, he was to be her husband. Better to start the way she intended to go on. With honesty.

"I find your face to be pleasing to the eye, my lord. You have kind eyes of a deep-ale brown. Your eyebrows are not too bushy. Your nose is not too long. Your chin is handsome without being too pointed, nor too short, nor too square. Your ears do not stick out. Your mouth . . ."

"My mouth?" he prompted, as she paused. He had smiled through all of her weighing of his features. Yet, for a mere moment, he looked serious.

"Does my mouth please you also, my lady?"

Augusta suddenly felt her own mouth go dry. She looked at his lips. They were the ones that would bestow her first grown-up kiss. They had no doubt kissed many another maiden, as she knew full well the life of a sailor was not a chaste one. How would he rate the untried kisses that she put against his lips?

Did his mouth please her? Well, it hadn't as yet, but she hoped it soon would.

She decided to skip the question.

"Perhaps we can also work on your attire."

"You seek to make me a dandy or a fop," Rolf said, coming another step closer. The smile was back on his face as he let his prior question go unanswered. "I assure you that is something I shall never be."

"Not a dandy, sir. But you are to be given control of Thornbury, upon the death of my father, and even before that, to be by his side and run the estate. Your heirs will be earls. Certainly, you don't want people to think that the lady of Thornbury has married beneath her and born her children to a man only fit to . . . to sail the seas and sit upon a horse."

His eyebrows had raised higher and higher during her speech. "*Ah*, now I understand. How I look reflects badly on you, is that it? Never mind that your knees are dirty and no doubt bruised about three times a day from your falls, or that your hair is oft unkempt from your tumbles down the stairs."

Augusta knew her cheeks were aflame with embarrassment. She had hoped that because Rolf had been away so much since his arrival, he hadn't noticed her penchant for clumsiness. She was abashed.

"I suppose Lady Brenville can slip and slide all over the place, as long as she has a clean face and hands," he continued, unmindful of her discomfort.

"Now, you are being cruel, sir."

"No," he began. "Rather, yes, I suppose I was. However, there is nothing wrong with fighting for one's king and country in the Royal Navy or sitting astride a horse to make a living as a soldier. In fact, Gus, I look forward to teaching you a thing or two about riding."

"I can ride a horse quite well, thank you," she lied, not wishing to add to his low opinion of her. "And what did you call me?"

"I called you Gus, and I wasn't talking about riding a horse." His eyes had captured hers and held them fast, as his meaning dawned on her.

"Oh," the word fell from her lips and nothing else came out.

"There," he said, closing the last steps between them. "We've had our first fight. And thus, we shall have the pleasure of making up."

She took a step backward and nearly tumbled over the other Rolf who was once more lying contentedly in the sun at her heels. As she flailed a moment, her betrothed grabbed her hand and yanked her upright, but she pulled her fingers free. "I was only trying to bring a little cleanliness into your life, my lord."

"I appreciate your concern," he said, closing the gap again and reaching for her. "And I think I'll appreciate even more than that."

His decision to seal their engagement with a kiss was so sudden, she couldn't help leaning away from him even as she closed her eyes in preparation. She felt the world tilt beneath her slippered feet. So this was the romantic sensation she'd been waiting for, this moving of the very earth beneath her. Then she realized that the ground really was tilting, and she was sliding backward down the bank of the river Thorn.

Grasping at Rolf, she tried to regain her footing, but it was too late. With her hands fisting his lapels, they crashed down into the cool water together, instantly both soaked from head to toe, and thrashing around to gain their footing.

In another moment, they faced each other staring in disbelief, standing in the thigh high water.

Mortified, Augusta was also more than a little angry. What did he mean advancing on her and attempting to take ungranted liberties with her person? Why, this latest inelegant mishap was certainly his fault, not hers.

Rolf seemed less than bothered. Chuckling, he shook his dark hair out of his eyes and then smoothed it back with both hands.

"Cleanliness you wanted, my lady, and cleanliness you have got."

Augusta was silent a moment, miserably combing a weed out of her own tangled hair with her fingers.

"If you had waited long enough," she said, gritting her teeth against the chilly waters, "I probably would have fallen in here by myself. You needn't have pushed me in."

His eyebrows shot up. Then he laughed at her interpretation of the event. And she was struck by the handsomeness of her husband-to-be when he laughed.

She narrowed her eyes. "But odds are, Captain Rolf, that you never would have taken a bath if not provoked to it," she concluded.

His laughter stopped.

"Shall I have a servant bring you some soap down here to the river," she continued, "or will the future master of Thornbury take his baths in a civilized manner up at the house with hot water?"

A grin spread across his face once more. "I don't think hot water will make your nipples hard as little rocks the way they are now, will it?"

"Oh!" Augusta gasped, far past blushing. Without thinking, she sank lower into the water to hide herself, but her feet slipped out from under her and her skirts pulled her down farther. She came up spluttering and clawing as she tried to stand. Before she could, Rolf's arms were around her, pulling her up and holding her steady.

"You needn't try to drown yourself, woman. I will take a damned bath and regularly, too. It was a luxury unavailable on-board ship, and I admit, I have fallen into a slovenly manner regarding it. Is that acceptable?"

As he asked his question, she felt his palm slip over her breast, so clearly outlined by her soaking dress. Her nipple throbbed as he brushed it. Standing stock still except for the shivering that was overtaking her, her eyes gazing down at the clear water around them instead of into his, she simply let him touch her.

Encouraged, his other hand took up a similar position on her other breast. She closed her eyes then, sucking in her breath and holding it while he caressed her tenderly. The cold water heightened the tingling that began between her legs. How could she feel so hot and so cold at the same time?

In truth, terror raced down her spine along with excitement, as she wondered what he would do next yet not wanting him to stop. This was the kind of pleasure that Millicent knew with her beau. And after Rolf was her husband, this was what was in store for her whenever it pleased him. Should she do something to him in return?

Finally, she let herself look up at his burnished brown eyes and found him waiting patiently. There was no smile on his face now as he moved his hands to her waist. With a small movement and with the help of the swirling water, he pulled her effortlessly off her feet and up against him. Her wet clothes bunched up between their bodies, yet still she could feel the whole length of him, chest to thighs.

"I think I like this method of bathing, Gus," he murmured, bending his head close to kiss her.

"Oohh!" shrieked Millie in her way. "Milady, are you all right?"

Augusta had not even noticed her approach. Sweet Mary, what had she seen?

Rolf was the first to move. He swept her up in his arms and carried her the couple steps to the bank where he deposited her. "You know your lady. She fell right in."

"Aye, it isn't the first time, is it, milady?" Millie slipped off her own cloak and put it around Augusta's shivering form.

Augusta was humiliated, both by having Millie find them in such a compromising situation and by having Rolf know that she *had* actually fallen into the stream before.

"I would like a hot bath," she said miserably, heading for the carriage that Millie had driven.

"I think I'll have one of those myself," Rolf added, the mirth obvious in his voice. "Your lady has convinced me of the pleasure of water, both hot and cold." He strode away from them toward his horse.

CHAPTER THREE

That night, soaking in a copper tub of steaming water, Rolf wondered if he'd moved too boldly, but then again, reflecting on the occurrence at the river, he decided he had not. He couldn't deny that he had wanted to explore more of his bride-to-be, and though Gus had been tentative, she had not rejected his advances.

She was clearly unskilled in anything remotely to do with the pleasures of fornication and that, in itself, excited him. He dunked his head under the water and came up spluttering. Then he scrubbed his arms and toes and thought some more.

He wasn't randy with lust for her, that was certain, but he found her appearance pleasing and her manner amusing. When he'd come upon her sitting beside the river, she'd looked downright enchanting. Perhaps it was because she had no artifice at all. Unaware of him, she had been sitting in a patch of late day sunshine, and it had brightened her hair and illuminated her intelligent face.

He'd suddenly wanted to kiss her. And he had almost succeeded. Moreover, he had enjoyed the feel of her body against his, albeit clad in water-soaked clothing, and also her warm, full breast in his hand. All in all, a good day.

Yes, he had congratulated himself more than once on the fates that had delivered him an estate, a manor, and a wife that all pleased him. All three worth every blasted shilling he was going to pour into them.

Standing up, he reached for a towel, admiring the handiwork of the bathing room in the flickering candlelight. He couldn't help grinning. If the fact that he hadn't had a woman in too long made him a tad forward with his bride, well, soon that wouldn't matter as the wedding rapidly approached. All his nervousness from the prior few weeks had disappeared. He rubbed his skin with the towel. He was most decidedly looking forward to being Gus's husband, to teaching her what he liked and disliked—in bed and out of it—and to having children of his own when the time came.

"Beg pardon, sir," Millicent said as she quickly bowed out of the bathing room before he'd even realized she'd come in. "I thought you were my mistress," she added through a crack in the door before she closed it firmly.

He stopped mid-drying, realizing his mouth was open in surprise, and then sat back down in the tub of now lukewarm water. Indeed, an honest mistake, he thought, given Gus's penchant for baths.

If anyone was in the bathing room splashing water around, it was likely to be her. Still, the thought of Gus's flaxen-haired maid caused him to grow hard instantly, even in the cooling water. Yes, it had been too long since he'd bedded a fair creature. Gus was going to be the lucky recipient of all his pent-up desire in a matter of a week.

He shook his hair, spraying the wall with water drops. However, if Gus turned out to be dry and prudish, then he would be happy indeed to have Millicent around. Only if she were willing, of course, and he imagined most of the women would be after he became master of the manor. Willing and at his disposal, so Gus had better please him in bed or he'd find a woman who would.

He laughed this time at the fanciful thoughts his new lofty station was affording him—fanciful and ridiculously foolish—and then he dunked his sailor's head under the water once more.

AUGUSTA HAD BEEN AVOIDING Rolf ever since the river incident. He had been so brazen, and she had thoroughly enjoyed it. Still, she was a noblewoman and a virgin and not yet married. In times such as these, with the threat of losing everything hanging over her head if it all didn't work out precisely as planned, she simply couldn't afford to lose her head . . . or her maidenhood—not until she was well and truly wedded.

After all, the captain was a stranger to her. Though his intentions seemed plain enough. He wanted a wife and her estate in exchange for his savings and income. But suppose he bedded her and then threatened to expose her lack of virginity in order to strike a better bargain? Though how he could gain more than being master of Thornbury and having his babes gain land and title was beyond her.

Still with the timing being so crucial, she would let nothing ruin their last hope.

Instead, she continued to run the estate, letting her father deal alone with the duties of being the local magistrate, and worrying far less than before about everything. Augusta used her free time to finish up plans for her wedding celebration and to dream of her wedding night. When it came time to speak with the local vicar about the ceremony, however, she saw only the man who had performed the funerals of three men dead because of her.

Thus it was, after not seeing Rolf for the better part of a day, she decided she'd better inform him of the mortal demise of three of her previous suitors, the most promising ones, the ones whom she hadn't had time to show the door.

Forewarned was forearmed, after all. Moreover, as he was her last chance to fulfill her grandfather's stipulations, Rolf needed to survive and do his husbandly duty.

It was no small task to find her betrothed, for he was everywhere at once, it seemed, and yet nowhere. He was interested in learning all he could about the tremendous task of running Thornbury, managing the Brenville legacy, understanding the condition of all things that would soon be under his command.

With her dog tagging along, Augusta searched the stables, but the head groom said the captain had left there an hour earlier. She went to the kitchens, only because her mouth watered at the smell of queen cakes. No doubt they'd been baked in little patty pans, and she couldn't resist sampling them. Then she tripped and fell on her way to seeing the groundskeeper. All to no avail. Rolf had been there and left.

She was still picking gravel out of her palms as she went to see the gamekeeper. After riding in her carriage to the mill, only to find that she had missed the infernal man from Kent by mere minutes, Augusta finally returned to the refuge of the king's solar, quite cross and exhausted.

Slamming the door behind her, and nearly catching her dog's tail in the process, she tossed her gloves down onto the nearest bench. Then she saw him, lounging . . . in her chair.

Immediately, Rolf began to bark, his hackles up.

"Exactly how I feel," Augusta muttered, though she patted her dog's head. "Ssh. It's alright."

"And what has you and your hound so disgruntled this lovely day?" asked Rolf, looking extremely relaxed with his boots up on her desk.

"For one thing, sir, I think you overstep your bounds. This is *my* solar."

He smiled, and it caused a quick fluttering in her belly. Despite the gap in his teeth, his smile was so disarming that she often found herself contemplating it in quiet moments.

He nodded, looking agreeable enough.

"So it is for now, my lady, but surely we will share it soon enough."

The sight of his long legs stretched out and his hands pressed behind his head did something strange to her stomach. After the wedding, his body would be stretching out next to hers. And even on top of hers. She swallowed.

Share a bed, she thought, yes, soon enough. Then she remembered what they were talking about.

"Soon enough," she agreed. Then it suddenly dawned on her. *Was he going to take over all that was hers?* Her bed, her solar, her body. She swallowed again. But think, dear Augusta, what you will get back.

"Yes, you're right, and I must get used to it. However, in the meantime," she said, as she walked over to him and knocked his legs aside, staring at the dirt that was left on the top of her usually pristine tabletop, "in the meantime, my lord, you will respect what is mine."

Rolf stared at her a minute. "I already do respect you, Gus, and all that you have accomplished here under less than desirable conditions."

Standing, he brushed the desk with his hand, which, she noted, he then wiped down the side of his trousers.

"I was merely waiting for you and taking a break. It has been a long day."

"As I found out," Augusta said, taking the seat he had just vacated. "I have been looking for you."

"Indeed, and I have been waiting here for you. Yet seeing your flushed cheeks and sparkling eyes, I confess it was worth the wait."

Her betrothed had just complimented her appearance. She didn't know what to reply, so she just patted Rolf's head until he lay on the threadbare rug.

The other Rolf rested his lean hips against her desk, right next to her, so she had to look up to see his face.

"I surmised," he added, "since I had seen so little of you these past days, that I must corner the fox in her own den."

A fox! Her? More like a mouse in its hole, she thought. But either way, he was the hunter.

"Why did you want to see me?" she asked, stalling the discussion of that which had caused her to seek him out, at the same time noticing that his gaze had dropped below her chin to her cleavage. Hunching over the desk, she traced lines on the ancient wood with her fingers.

"Do I need a reason to see my bride?" he asked.

She looked up at him again to see if he was teasing, narrowing her eyes in answer. He laughed.

"I have spoken to many people these past days, and I have learned quite a bit, but when I try to delve deeper, I find my questions stymied and the same response always given, 'Ask Lady Augusta.' Either you are the ultimate authority on all the workings of Thornbury, or the people simply don't trust me."

"The answer, Captain Rolf," she said without false humility and purposefully ignoring the dog's barking response, "is no doubt a bit of both. You cannot expect to become an expert on my home in a matter of days, nor even weeks, when it has taken me a lifetime."

He was undaunted. "Then I think we should ride out together so that everyone sees I am your chosen husband, and not some unwanted suitor. What, my lady? What is wrong?" he asked, reaching for her hand as she gasped at his choice of words.

The dog jumped up from his place at her feet and started to growl at Rolf again.

"Rolf, be still," she snapped, her nerves tense at the thought of the three dead men. The dog settled back down while his namesake dropped his hold on her hand, a look of utmost surprise upon his face.

My, that works well, she thought. *Two Rolfs silenced and held at bay with one command.* But she owed the human one an explanation, particularly as she had just given him a sharp rebuke.

"In case you have not realized it, my hound's name is precisely the same as your own."

His raised eyebrows, his shocked expression, both indicated he had not known.

She demonstrated. "Rolf," she said, her voice gentle. The dog lifted its head and gazed adoringly at her. She looked to her betrothed who was looking more horrified than adoring. She shrugged.

"If I thought the dog smart enough to learn a new one at this stage, I would try, but verily, my lord, it would be easier if you changed yours." She offered him a smile.

As his face flushed and his surprise turned to displeasure, her smile froze, feeling plastered upon her face. *Foolish woman,* she berated herself.

"Oh dear," she murmured, as clumsy in her humor as in everything else. "I am jesting with you, my lord. You have a fine name. Obviously, I think so, elsewise I would not have given it to . . . my dog."

She stopped and took a deep breath. It was time to divulge what was really causing her nerves to fray and her shoe to be practically wedged into her mouth with each indecorous statement. "I have been looking for you all morning," she said again, "because I thought you ought to know that you are, perhaps, in grave danger, and mayhap you will be even more so if we start riding out together." Never mind the fact that she might fall off her horse and leave her intended bereaved before the wedding.

ROLF FROWNED DOWN AT his bride. She had a knack for surprising him, keeping him on edge, and he wasn't sure he liked it or would get used to such. In truth, his name had been a sore spot when he was a lad, an antiquated appellation, a fanciful notion of his mother to label him a medieval knight.

Yet nothing would make him discount a word Gus said, about danger or anything else. Her ability to run Thornbury with the capability of an admiral over his navy had proven her to be an intelligent and apt female.

Thus, he asked her, "In danger? From whom?"

"I fear that you have been partly deceived by my father in that he chose to leave out something you may find particularly off-putting in our contract of marriage. I have had three men agree to be my husband."

He thought he kept his expression one of neutrality, but she looked instantly miffed.

"Yes, Captain, believe it or not, three suitors have asked for my hand."

"No, my lady, you mistake me," he assured her. Time to be gallant, he decided. "I am not surprised by the number, except as how it is triflingly few."

Though truth be told, a feeling akin to amazement washed over him that three men had agreed to bail out the sagging Brenville fortunes, seeing that Augusta, though fair of face, was not exceptional in her beauty. "And why did you turn down these suitors?"

She swallowed, visibly ill at ease. "That's the thing. I did not turn them down. I mean, perhaps I would have if given the chance."

"I have lost the path of our discussion," he confessed.

"They died, my lord, before I could turn them down or get to the altar."

"Died?" he repeated, watching her cheeks grow flushed.

"Yes, all three," she paused and absently stroked the hound's head, "and by what some might say are mysterious circumstances."

Ah. Rolf had the answer to something that had plagued him for the past couple of days.

"So that is the Brenville curse. I had heard of it from the locals, just a muttering here and there, but could not discover what it was. I think your townsfolk are as desirous to have you married and to save the manor as you are." He couldn't help laughing.

"You laugh at this curse?"

"Only because I was starting to think it was your . . ." He snapped his mouth closed and stared at her, trying to think of something to fill the terrible silence. What was he thinking! Clod! Imbecile!

"My what?" Her eyes were wide, dark pools of brandy, gazing up at him.

He couldn't finish his sentence and say "your clumsiness." How utterly insensitive that he'd nearly said it aloud, but he had found nothing cursed here except her inability to stay on her own two feet.

"Your . . . your lack of sheep," he finished lamely.

She opened her mouth, then closed it. After a moment, she asked, "Our lack of sheep?"

"Yes, for such a pastoral place, I would have thought you would have more. Sheep, I mean."

"Well, my lord," she said, standing up, looking as though she might be questioning his intelligence, "perhaps when you are master here, you can set yourself upon this sheep matter. I'll leave it to you to sort out."

She paced across the room, and with each step, he practically held his breath awaiting the inevitable tumble over a nonexistent obstacle on the old carpet.

"Still, the death of three men is nothing to take lightly. My father is certain they were killed, one perhaps poisoned and the other two found with arrows in their backs."

He coughed. "Yes, that would be considered more than mysterious circumstances, my lady. I would say your father is quite correct, for I have seen some terrible archers but none who were able to mortally wound themselves in their own backs."

"I suppose you are correct. However, since the only connection among the three were their desire to marry me, I had hoped I was not the cause of three horrendous murders."

"Undoubtedly so," he sympathized. "The villain is most likely whoever stands to gain Thornbury and the rest of the Brenville estate if you don't produce an heir."

She stopped and blushed again. "You know about my grandfather's will?"

"Your father spoke to me about the will even before I agreed to marry you. I know, for instance, that we will need to beget an heir rather quickly, and thus will be busy from our wedding night onward."

She ceased her infernal pacing, and he watched as her face flamed scarlet. He felt almost wicked for teasing her. Almost. For she also started to breathe in short nervous intakes that caused her full breasts to rise and fall quite delightfully.

Because of that, he added, "I don't mind if we start early."

"Oh dear," she exclaimed. Then, when he smiled, she laughed as if he were joking, her hand fluttering to her throat.

In truth, each day, he found he wanted his betrothed just a little bit more and found the wedding night seemed too long to wait. It was long past time to kiss her and let her know what pleasures awaited.

Before he could act, she turned on her heel and paced to the other end of the room.

"Let us focus on the matter at hand, my lord. You are sensible in thinking the next heir would have reason to kill off my suitors, but that would be my cousin Wesley. You'll meet him soon. You'll meet all the family soon, of course. Wesley and I have ever been upon friendly terms. I know in my heart that he would not harm me."

"But what about harming your prospective husband?"

She shook her head. "He is simply not the type. Wesley is open and sweet."

Rolf raised an eyebrow at her testimonial.

"No, honestly," she went on, "we played together as children, along with his younger brother, James. Wesley is intelligent and kind, and he always makes me laugh."

"He sounds like a paragon of virtue. I'm surprised you're not marrying *him*. All your problems regarding your grandfather's will would vanish in one fell swoop." Rolf couldn't keep the edge out of his voice, which he recognized—to his annoyance—as jealousy over the way Gus prattled on about her cousin.

She ignored his tone. "He has never asked me. Besides, I think of him more as a brother."

He didn't like the fact that she hadn't denied that marriage to Wesley would have been agreeable to her.

"Perhaps he wants Thornbury very much, and you are simply in the way.'"

"No," she said firmly, shaking her head. "He could never kill someone. He is not vile and cruel . . ."

She trailed off , no doubt due to the expression on his face. He couldn't help the surge of irritation he felt.

"What?" she asked.

"I have killed men, Gus. Do you think me vile and cruel?"

Instantly, she looked contrite, no doubt realizing how she'd offended him.

"No, my lord. I have no reason to think you either of those traits." She closed the distance once more. "It's true that I don't know you well, but you have a kind smile, and you have been respectful to my father and . . . gentle with me. Why, this very day, the estate staff spoke highly of your demeanor."

He felt himself growing uncomfortable at her words. Yet he'd childishly cast his line into the water, fishing for these very compliments.

He shrugged. "Don't paint me as a saint, Gus. I am a fighting man when called upon, though I am happy to put down my weapons, too. Except in the face of this threat to our safety—"

"Not mine, just yours, I fear. No one has ever tried to harm me."

"That may be," he agreed, "but with the wedding so close, anything could happen if someone is truly trying to keep you from producing an heir. It might be better if you didn't walk out alone until after the wedding, perhaps until after the birth of our first born."

There was that pretty rosy-colored flush upon her tanned cheeks, no doubt brought on by his reminding her that certain acts would take place to beget a child.

"You look lovely when you blush," he told her, as she pressed her palms against her face with embarrassment. And he was surprised to realize that he meant it. She did indeed look lovely, with her hair down and windswept and her eyes glittering back at him as he teased her. He stepped closer. They had nearly kissed in the river, and he'd been thinking about how she'd looked, with her face turned up to him waiting for his lips. He'd wanted to find her any number of times over the past couple of days and finish what they'd started before Millie had interrupted them.

He wrapped one arm around her slender waist and pulled her toward him a mere moment before the door flew open. They both looked at her father, who didn't seem the least upset to find them in an embrace. Rather, his startled expression met theirs, as if he'd never thought of his daughter in a romantic position before. Briefly, his forehead wrinkled like the dog's, then it smoothed.

"So, you two are getting along well, eh?"

Rolf bit back his words of frustration. Could he simply kiss the woman once, for Christ's sake? Instead, he felt Gus step back, turning to the elder Brenville.

"Is anything wrong, Father?"

"No, dear, just thought I'd let you know that a messenger has arrived from your cousins. They'll be here on the morrow, by midday."

Augusta looked at Rolf.

"Wesley?" he asked.

"Yes, and his brother, James, and his wife, Helen, with their children."

If a threat to his marriage day, not to mention his gaining control of Thornbury, was about to descend upon them in the form of Wesley Brenville, then he'd best be prepared.

"I'll let you see to readying guest rooms and such, Gus. I must speak with Perry." He was gone without a backward glance.

"A bit of an abrupt fellow," her father commented. "And what did he call you?"

Augusta just sighed. It seemed as if the road to the altar and to her first kiss was a long one indeed.

CHAPTER FOUR

Rolf found Perry near the stables, shirtless and sweaty and holding his fighting sword. He was exercising in the yard with the help of one of the groom's, who was trying to keep up by waving a broom handle toward Perry when yelled at to do so. Rolf stripped off his own shirt and motioned for the groom to move away. With a grateful nod, he did so.

Within moments, Rolf drew his own sword, it's fluted handle fitting perfectly in his hand. For silent moments, they parried and thrust in turn, Rolf concentrating on nothing else except their practiced movements and hearing only Perry's answering grunts.

Yet after a little while, Gus slipped into his mind, and he found himself thinking of her sweet expression, of her gently curving hips that he'd rested his hands upon, of her pale pink lips that she seemed willingly to offer him.

"Rolf." He heard his name but ignored it for a moment, imagining a wedding night that would happen very soon.

"Rolf."

He hated having his concentration broken, then he suddenly realized that Perry had stopped his workout and now rested his sword, point down, while Rolf continued to swish at the air.

"What has you in such a state that you nearly killed me?"

"Nearly killed . . . what do you mean?"

"For a moment, your onslaught was anything but practice."

Rolf realized he was breathing hard and the sweat was running down his back. Apparently, thoughts of Gus had sent him into frustrated distraction.

"My apologies," he offered, wiping a hand over his brow. "Wedding guests are arriving by tomorrow night, and we must be ready for anything. Have you heard of the Brenville curse?"

Perry made a face. "Aye, three dead men."

How in blazes had Perry discovered that before him? Rolf reached for his shirt, wiped the sweat off himself with it, and then carelessly put it back on.

"It stands to reason that the killer gains by Gus remaining a maid."

"Agreed," Perry said. "We'd best stick close to your lady then. A dead maid stays a maid."

It wasn't the first time that Rolf was pleased to have the likes of Lieutenant Peregrine Newbury at his side. Perry had a quick grasp and good aim with both sword and pistol. There was no one whom he would trust with Gus's life more than Perry except himself.

"How many are coming to this fete of yours?" Perry asked, as they headed inside for a drink.

Rolf shrugged. "I know not."

"And your family?"

Rolf shook his head. "There isn't time, nor need. They'll come next year, maybe to celebrate an heir, or to enjoy the estate in its summer glory."

"Eager to show off your prize."

Rolf smiled. That went without saying. Thornbury exceeded even his own family's home. "Yes," he admitted, "but I'll also enjoy the company of family. You know as well as I that Garth won't believe it until he sees for himself that his brother has done well."

Perry laughed and clapped him on the shoulder.

"In any case," Rolf continued, "I want to put a stop to this blasted 'curse' nonsense before my family comes anywhere near. But I'm taking it seriously, and you must watch over Gus whenever I'm not available."

"That I will," Perry agreed. "And it will be a pleasure."

Rolf looked at him with narrowed eyes. "What do you mean by that?"

Perry grinned at his friend's expression, then he shrugged seeing that he was serious. "I meant what I said. It will be a pleasure. Your lady has above-average intelligence. For a woman, I mean, and she can converse on many subjects. Perhaps she'll be of use in picking me out a bride of my own. Besides, she makes everyone around her feel happy. Have you not noticed?"

Rolf frowned. Hearing his future wife's attributes reported in glowing terms by another man, even his best friend, was disconcerting. He was indeed lucky to be marrying Gus. He had noticed her intelligence and her effect on the household, especially himself. She made him want to spend more time with her. In fact, the longer he was there, the more he wanted to see her and the more his longing for the marriage bed grew.

"Less than a week to go," he mused aloud.

Perry roared with laughter, knowing where his friend's thoughts had gone.

"THIS SEEMS UNNECESSARY," AUGUSTA was saying for what seemed like the hundredth time as Perry rode his horse close beside her wagon. In fact it was like having two dogs everywhere she went, with her hound on one side and the impressive lieutenant on the other. She had ridden out to inspect a barn fire in the town that thankfully had caused the death of neither animal nor person.

After that, she'd paid a promised call to the vicar, then the chandler who was working overtime to make sure there were enough candles for the wedding and the celebration that would follow. Through it all, Perry had remained discreetly but determinedly beside her.

"Rolf wants nothing to happen to you. Nor do I."

Augusta blushed pink with pleasure. In actuality, she had never felt so cared for in her life, even if the motives were clearly not sentimental.

"Well, that makes three of us," she said, as they crested a hill in the late afternoon sun. "Here's the spot I was thinking of. I always thought it would be a lovely place to have a house. There is good water from the stream yonder, and the land doesn't flood even in the hardest rains. See there, there are already plentiful wild berry bushes. And the view—it is one of the prettiest in the area. You can see almost to Salisbury . . ."

But Perry clearly had stopped listening. He had dismounted and was touching the soil. Then he turned in a slow circle, allowing his gaze to take in the horizon in every direction. In a few moments, he had been down to the stream and tasted the water. Then he came back to Augusta, smiling broadly.

"It is just as you said, and all I could wish for. I will buy it off of you, Lady Augusta, at a fair price."

"I will sell it to you, Lieutenant, at an even fairer price. As my husband's friend, and I hope soon to be mine as well, you honor us by choosing to stay close."

"The honor is mine," Perry said.

They turned their horses back toward Thornbury, where Rolf, even in the absence of the actual marriage, was already paying men to go about fixing the small things that could be easily done before the wedding guests arrived. The garden had been cleaned up of all debris and any cracked windows replaced.

As they approached her home along the cart road to the yew gardens, Augusta felt a shiver of excitement run down her spine: lovely Thornbury would be restored.

Entering through the newly renovated gate of solid oak instead of patched boards, she noticed the Brenville flag was flying high over the main octagonal tower. She squealed, clapping her hands in delight. The last banner had broken free during a storm and they had never replaced it.

She pointed it out to her escort.

"This is so exciting," she said, turning to look at Perry upon horseback.

"I think your future husband has some surprises in store inside as well," he said.

"Really?" Augusta couldn't wait. She jumped down from the wagon seat, at the same time hearing Perry shout her name, a tone of caution in his voice. In another moment, he was beside her, having dismounted in a rush to remain her vigilant guard.

Practically running in her haste to see what Rolf had accomplished in her absence, Augusta felt her boot make contact with a larger stone in the crushed stone path, a familiar feeling that always heralded a tumble. Sure enough, she stumbled and fell to her knees. As she went down, she heard a strange whizzing in the air, then another. For a moment she thought a large bird had come flying close by. Then she heard the lieutenant groan, and from her place on the ground, she watched him collapse on his hands and knees beside her. At the same instant, her dog seemed to become a lunatic, barking loudly and running agitatedly back and forth before picking up an arrow that had appeared on the ground directly in front of her.

Confused, Augusta reached out to Perry, only to see an arrow sticking out of his side. In another moment, and rather slowly, he lay himself down on his stomach. Augusta watched the blood flow from his wound, disbelieving what she was seeing. But before she could speak, a shadow chased her away from his side. She rolled clear just as Perry's large horse nearly trod on her, coming to stand over its master as it had been trained.

"Perry?" she said from a few feet away, feeling helpless for the first time that she could remember.

"My lady, stay low." His voice was so quiet, she could barely hear him. "Crawl under the wagon until help comes."

He said not another word. Yet still he breathed, she noted, albeit shallowly.

She did not do as she was told and hide under the wagon like a child. This was her home, and, even with terror raging through her brain and her body, she was thinking of how to get to safety and bring help for her new friend.

"Rolf," she called, bringing her dog to her side. Hooking her hand in his collar, she crouched beside him, hoping to be forgiven for using her beloved hound as a shield. Moving swiftly, they ran together toward the first bisecting path and then farther, to the arched Tudor door of rough-hewn oak. On her knees, she pounded on this. In a moment, it opened and she looked up into the craggy face of Peter Moon, who had cared for their gardens for his whole life.

"Milady?" his face was one of astonishment to see his mistress crouching at his feet, holding her dog.

"One of our guests has been gravely injured. He is even now lying in the first quadrant of the yew garden."

Hearing the urgency in her voice, the man called behind him, "David, come at once." And both sets of legs ran past her.

The dog barked and tugged at her hold on him, clearly wanting to run with them. She heard a noise and realized she was sobbing.

"Stop it," she scolded herself, as well as Rolf, tugging at his collar to obey while wiping at her tears with her sleeve.

Rolf! She must locate him immediately.

Within minutes—although it seemed like an hour had passed—she was in Perry's chamber, holding his cold hand and listening for her betrothed's footsteps. She'd waited for David and Peter to come by carrying Perry, and had decided to stay with him. Calling for others to find Rolf, she'd accompanied the wounded man indoors, right to his chamber. Here, after issuing orders to get the surgeon, she'd waited.

The door burst open, causing Augusta to jump as Rolf entered at a run. She could feel the fear emanating from him. Squeezing Perry's hand, she stood when her future husband reached the bedside. His stricken expression at seeing his friend laid low nearly caused her tears to flow again.

"If I hadn't fallen, it would be me," she voiced the words that had been going over and over in her mind in the silence of the chamber. "I'm truly sorry."

Rolf tore his gaze from Perry and looked at her as if he didn't understand her, then he nodded and returned his attention to his friend.

"He has been in and out of sleep since we brought him here," she told him, when still Rolf said nothing.

Again, he nodded, before reaching down to remove the linen sheet that she had wadded into a ball and pressed against Perry's wound. The arrow still stuck out, quivering with every shallow breath that he took. Now he groaned, and Rolf pressed the rag back into place with a firm hand.

Augusta watched his actions. Did Rolf blame her for his friend's plight? Would he have preferred that it had been her? Shame washed over her for wondering such selfish thoughts when Perry could die. As the guilt and sadness and helplessness all swirled in her head, she knew she would do anything to help set things right.

Then Rolf looked round at her as if reading her thoughts, and she was grateful that his eyes did not seem in the least condemning.

"Do you have a surgeon hereabouts?" he asked, his voice sounding strangely old and spiritless. She hugged her arms around her.

"A good one, so I'm told, in Bristol. I've already sent for him. We have a barber in town," Augusta added, less than enthusiastically. Then she had an idea. "While we wait for the surgeon, I know a far more skilled healer."

"Then send for him," Rolf said.

Her," Augusta corrected and frowned for a moment. Yes, that's what she must do, locate Bernadine. She hurried to the doorway to find the grim-faced groundskeeper, Peter, who'd been told to wait for more instructions. She noted the blood still on his shirt and hands, and her stomach convulsed.

"You must take me to the forest, and we must go now."

"Yes, milady," Peter said.

Before they could take a step, Rolf's voice stopped her. "No." His footsteps came up swiftly behind her. "I won't have you shot down as well. It's too dangerous. Why can't the man go alone?"

Augusta opened her mouth to argue and restrained herself just in time. Rolf was right after all, at least about her going out. It was certainly not the time to get herself killed. However, Rolf did not understand the circumstances.

"He will never be able to find Bernadine by himself. She lives a somewhat gypsy-like existence, and Kilnore Woods is secretive at the best of times."

Augusta had been welcomed into its heart more than once due to her charitable gifts and because Bernadine was Millie's sister. But Peter . . . he would need—

"Take a female with you," Augusta said. "Millicent is not here at present, but take Abby with you, Abby from the kitchens," she added, "not upstairs Abby."

"I can find her," Peter scoffed, sounding annoyed, "with or without Abby, milady."

She turned back to the groundskeeper. He'd lived in the area all his life and knew everyone. And for most of those, he cared not a whit. He was a gruff, grumpy old man, but she'd seen him carry Perry with the utmost care.

"Take Abby," she ordered him. "Bernadine will balk otherwise, but make sure to say she comes at my personal behest."

"Aye, milady."

Peter was already bowing and heading down the hallway, understanding the urgency.

"Make sure Bernadine brings whatever she needs to tend a wounded man," she called after him. "And go with all due haste."

"Aye, milady." He disappeared out of sight.

All they could do now was wait and pray. If their relationship had been closer, Augusta would have taken Rolf's hand in hers and held it, and perhaps held him, too. Instead, she gave him an encouraging smile and went to sit vigil with him at Perry's bedside.

In the quiet, she heard the horn heralding the arrival of someone newly come to Thornbury.

HOURS LATER, THE SIGHT that met Rolf's eyes was nearly as shocking to him as the earlier one of Perry, lying ashen-faced and bleeding. Now, he walked into the great hall to find his bride in the arms of another man. A tall, blond, decidedly well-groomed man. Rolf felt instant hatred and knew at once that this must be Wesley. The man was so clean, he was practically shining.

He watched the pair who had their arms around each other and their faces close together in discussion. Augusta's body was relaxed and her features were animated though unsmiling. Obviously telling her cousin about her harrowing adventure, Rolf thought.

As for Wesley, he was all concern and sympathy. Rolf had yet to digest his own feelings about his bride's narrow escape that might cost him his best friend's life. However, that would wait until later. Still, the couple hadn't noticed him, so he strode over with loud footfalls.

When he reached them, he wanted to say something that would claim her and all of Brenville as his own, something witty and droll, something that would make Wesley take his damn hands immediately off of Gus and that would make Perry laugh later when he related the discourse.

"You must be Wesley," was all that came out of his mouth, sounding peevish and insecure. To his amazement, neither seemed to observe his own lack of grace. Gus, having already turned at the sound of his steps, placed her soft hand on his forearm.

"How is the lieutenant at present?" she asked, genuine concern lacing her tone.

Together, Rolf and Gus had remained in silence with Perry until Bernadine had arrived. Every bit as beautiful as her sister, Millicent, she'd proven to be exactly what Gus had claimed, a skillful healer. Soon, the woman had removed the arrow and staunched the fresh flow of blood that her action had necessarily caused.

Then Rolf had sent Gus away while he kept vigil as Bernadine used her poultices and potions to ease his pain and keep infection at bay.

"He's sleeping again, thanks to the healer."

"Fever?" Gus asked with a furrowed brow that he wanted to smooth with his thumb. But he didn't..

He shook his head. "Not yet."

"Thank God," she added.

Yes, thank God, that's what he'd said many times in the past few hours. He'd thanked God that Perry was still alive despite the blood loss, and he'd thanked God for sparing Gus. If someone had to battle for life, he was glad it was his strong, battle-tried friend and not his blushing bride. He couldn't imagine standing helpless and seeing an arrow protruding from her smooth skin. He shuddered at the image in his head.

She squeezed his arm, thinking his thoughts must be all on Perry.

He gave her back almost a smile. She had a good heart and seemed to really care whether his friend lived or died. She had looked so scared and so . . . different. Gus with her hair all a tangle and her clothes covered in dirt from crawling to get help for Perry.

She had cleaned herself up to meet their guests, and looked lovely in a green gown that set off the chestnut tones of her hair.

"I, too, am so sorry to hear of these unhappy tidings," said a smooth voice. "Especially on what should be a festive occasion."

Rolf had nearly forgotten Wesley. Nearly.

"Yes," Rolf said, "how unfortunate that the murder attempt coincided with your arrival. It does put a damper on the merriments."

Gus gasped.

Rolf inwardly chastised himself. Perhaps he'd been a bit forward and harsh. However, the image of Gus so close to this man who could very well have ordered her death galled him no end.

Wesley swallowed once and pursed his lips. Then, to Rolf's surprise he nodded. "I understand how this must upset you. Augusta has told me how close you are to your friend. And it is unfortunate that the incident has cast suspicion on me and my household, for Augusta and I are close, too, and I would very much like to be here on her wedding day."

Rolf rolled his eyes. The man was too much, really. But he tried not to sneer and instead said, "You may stay, Wesley, but you will be watched." And with that, he strode away without even a by-your-leave.

He went to the sitting room that looked out over the front of the estate. Gus had told him it was where she was sitting when she first saw him riding up to

Thornbury. Once inside the room, he poured himself a drink. If only Perry were up and about so they could discuss the very thing that caused him not to be up and about. And now he would have to guard Gus himself every moment that she was outside of the manor. Not to mention keeping an eye on Wesley.

Rolf drained his glass. He needed backup in the worst way. Perhaps he would send for some of his shipmates. In the meantime, he could rely on Lord Brenville, he supposed, though he certainly couldn't ask the old man to keep an eye on cousin Wesley. After all, they were blood family.

Then Rolf sat down to wait with his legs stretched out in front of him and a refreshed drink in his hand. He knew it wouldn't be long before the inevitable storm entered the room in the form of an enraged Gus.

Sure enough, within a few minutes, his betrothed had tracked him down as expected. The door swung inward with such vehemence that even the heavy curtains swished with the force of her entry. Naturally, Rolf, the dog, followed dutifully behind.

"How could you be so rude to my cousin?" she asked, coming to stand before him, hands on her hips.

When he said nothing, but merely took a swig from his drink, she actually stamped her foot, which he found charming. Still, he winced for how close she came to treading on her hound's tail. He watched her take a deep breath.

"I have told you Wesley is above reproach. He is good and kind and . . ."

Rolf let her go on with her tirade about the virtues of Wesley. He leaned farther back in the armchair and closed his eyes.

"You are not even listening to me," she said at last.

"No, I'm not." He opened his eyes and fixed her with his gaze. "For nothing you say and certainly nothing that simpering fool says will convince me of anything. Only finding the would-be assassin will tell us the truth. And that's what I will spend my time doing. By the way, where is the rest of Wesley's family?"

She didn't answer at first, then she lowered her arms to her sides and sighed.

"He said they will arrive tomorrow or the next day. My understanding is that James's wife was indisposed temporarily," she began in quieter tones. "Wesley has just informed me that she's expecting another baby. Their other two children will stay at home anyway: Randall, my nephew, and Christine, my niece. They are dear little ones who . . ."

She trailed off when Rolf waved his hand for her to leave out the details.

"Who else?" he asked.

"Another cousin, Lloyd, on my mother's side is off buying horseflesh somewhere in the north, but Father expects he will arrive soon."

"If not," Rolf said, "he'll miss the wedding."

"And Cousin Walter is expected today, but you are acquainted with him already."

Rolf nodded, recalling the kindly older man who had sought him out regarding the marriage contract on Lord Brenville's behalf.

"My Aunt Mathilda may make it, and if she does, she'll bring Aunt Elizabeth. They will both arrive on the morrow, or so my father believes unless we get a missive telling us otherwise."

They sounded like a safe pair. He sipped his drink. The most likely perpetrator was still Wesley.

"What about *your* family?" she asked, and he thought, not for the first time, how little they really knew about each other.

"None can attend."

"Oh." She looked taken aback.

"It's not that they disapprove of this marriage," he began. How could they, when they knew so little about it? He rubbed his thumb up and down the flagon's side.

"If we were having a longer engagement, I'm sure they would all attend. Well, maybe not *all* of them . . ."

He shrugged. "I don't care to go into the whole story of my family right now. I'm sure your father has all the information in a letter somewhere. He did plenty of checking into my background from what I can gather. Why don't you ask him?"

Her eyes opened wide. "I was not meaning to pry, Captain Rolf."

He'd hurt her feelings, he realized belatedly. However, getting into the details of his oft-overbearing older brother and his bossy sister—well, he was simply too damnably stressed already.

"I'm sorry, Gus. Another day, we'll discuss every member of my branch of the family and the entire tree if you like. Just not now. I'll even take you on a post-wedding trip to meet them and then you can see my home. However, at present, let's concentrate on becoming man and wife, shall we?"

"About our wedding," she ventured, still looking piqued. "What about Perry?"

"The wedding will go on as scheduled. It must. I'm sure Perry will be well enough to sit and watch, even if he can't stand by my side," Rolf assured her though he was not sure of that at all.

"The sooner we consummate the marriage," he paused as she blushed a lovely shade of pink, "and start creating an heir," he paused again as she went red as a beet, "the better it will be, although I fear your freedom will have to be severely restricted from now on."

He could tell by her mutinous face that she didn't like the sound of that.

"Before you start to argue, Gus, just remember that Perry lies wounded. If you hadn't tripped, it would be you, probably dead for the arrow would have hit you higher in the chest."

He swallowed thickly at the thought. Arrows were for soldiers and deer, not for women. He looked at her again and drained the last drops from the crystal before setting it on the table.

"I don't want a repeat of today for any reason."

"Nor do I," she said, all the vehemence gone from her speech. She sounded merely tired. "However, have you thought that maybe I was not the target, that Perry really was the intended victim? As I've told you before, *I* have never been threatened. My other suitors died without me anywhere near."

"I have thought of that," he told her. "If it is true, then the archer was aiming for me. And if so, the killer is someone who thought Perry was your betrothed, someone then, not of this household, someone like Wesley."

She threw her arms up. "Not that again," she said.

"Yes, that again," he said, coming toward her. "I don't know yet if your cousin is a threat, but we'll treat him as such for now. And while he is under suspicion, I don't want you to be alone with him."

"That's ridiculous," she began, but as he closed the distance between them, she started to back up.

Rolf caught her hand in his and then her other hand. At arm's length, for a long moment, they stared at each other, and he felt every ounce of pent-up anger and anxiety. Then she blinked, and he felt her soften. He smiled slightly and pulled her close, as he'd wanted to do all day, feeling her heartbeat against his chest. She was safe. This could have been a terrible day, the worst in his life in fact.

"Rolf?" she asked, looking up at him.

He stared down into her puzzled nut-brown eyes. Was she asking him if he cared for her?

"Yes," he told her, even if she had no idea what his meaning was. He was about to tell her how quickly it seemed that he had become fond of her when a horn in the courtyard told them that someone else was arriving. He'd heard it once already today when Wesley arrived, and now, he had the feeling that more trouble would follow.

"Let's go find out who has come," he told her, relieved that the horn had stopped him from saying any more. Easily he spun her around, urging her out the sitting room door ahead of him.

Gus had taken but a few steps along the hall when she stumbled and he caught her elbow, hauling her up again. They both looked down to see what she'd tripped on. Merely a lace cap, the kind any number of waiting ladies or even a lady's maid would wear.

Bending down, Rolf picked it up and handed it to her.

"How odd," she said, fingering the fine workmanship of the lace.

"What?" he asked. "It's just a cap, is it not?"

"True, yet I've never seen anything like it before. It doesn't belong to Millie, nor to any of the servants of the manor, as far as I know."

He felt a chill chase down his spine. Someone had been in the hallway, perhaps lurking outside the open doorway. He frowned. To what purpose? Perhaps to listen to their conversation.

"Why don't you keep it tucked away until we can discern its owner. Moreover, speak of it to no one," he told her.

She nodded, not questioning. He knew Gus was smart and grasped the need for secrecy. He watched with interest as she tucked the scrap of lace down the front of her bodice between her breasts. It disappeared from view, yet his eyes remained rooted to the spot until she spoke.

"Shall we go?" she asked.

He detected a trace of satisfaction at the attention she'd aroused, and he had to admit that wasn't all that had been aroused at the sight of her fingertips disappearing between her cleavage. He shook his head.

"No?" she said, arching an eyebrow.

"Yes," he said, "let's go."

She walked in front of him with a saucy sway of her hips that made him smile. Not once did she trip or stumble or even hesitate as they made their way downstairs.

CHAPTER FIVE

When Rolf had endured all he could of the latest wedding guest's arrival, elder Brenville's cousin, Walter Montmorency from Sittingbourne, he went upstairs to check on Perry.

Quietly, he pushed the door to the chamber open. The room was darkened, but he could make out the form of Bernadine, sitting beside the bed in a comfortable chair, her eyes closed, a book clasped in her hands. The remains of a food tray were beside her feet on the floor.

Rolf hesitated. Was she sleeping along with her patient?

"Come in, my lord," she said softly at the same moment that her eyes opened.

He was momentarily transfixed by her glittering green gaze, illuminated from the light that spilled in behind him, as was her flaxen hair. His foolish thoughts imagined her more witch than healer. He banished them.

"I awakened you," he began, about to apologize, but she shook her head.

"Nay, I was just going over a passage I'd read earlier, and seeing if I remembered it all precisely."

"Really?" He was amazed that the young woman from the forest could read at all.

"Yes, *really*," and she laughed, clearly undisturbed by his surprise at finding her learned.

Rolf smiled wryly. So far, he agreed Gus's suggestion to bring Bernadine had been an excellent one. So similar in looks to her younger sister, she was yet as different in nature from Millie as night from day. Where Millicent was flighty and loud, Bernadine had a quiet strength about her. Where Millie was openness and light, every expression plain on her face, Bernadine seemed closed and mysterious. She'd swept into the bedchamber with a calm certainty, and Rolf had felt assured by her presence. She had spoken scarcely a word from that moment on. Instead, she had got right down to work, removing the arrow gently and treating the wound.

Now, he discovered the lady could talk after all, and read, and laugh. But could she heal?

"How is he?" Rolf walked over to his friend's bed. Perry appeared to be merely in normal sleep.

She put the book down on a table nearby and stood next to Rolf.

"He drifts in and out of wakefulness in what I believe is a healing sleep. It has been hours since the arrow pierced him, yet so far, no fever. That's a good sign. Now what he needs is rest. I believe the body actually makes blood, replenishing what is lost and sleep is the best time for that to happen.

She looked up at Rolf, perhaps expecting him to shrug off her theory, or worse, discount her out of hand.

Instead, he nodded. "I believe you are right. I have read nothing on medicine. It has never interested me, but I've seen enough on the battlefield to know that it only makes sense that a body makes new blood, otherwise, one would be forever as weak as the moment one suffers the wound and initial loss. You literally see the color drain out of a man along with his blood and likewise, color comes back in due course. Surely, that must be the time it takes to make new blood. We had a barber with the troops in the army, along with a physician, of course. The barber swore by warm broth to speed the healing, perhaps the warmth helped new blood to develop."

He shrugged now, quite out of his realm, but he was rewarded with a smile from Bernadine.

"I too have found warm liquids help in the healing. Whether it be a new mother or a wounded man. In fact, I've just sent a servant to bring up some broth. I thought that at Perry's next waking, I would trickle what I can into his mouth along with elderberry and echinacea tea that I know speed healing."

To Rolf's surprise, she bent down, close to Perry and brushed the hair back from his forehead.

"He is a strong man," she said quietly. "He should not die from an unseen coward's hand." Then she ran her hand across his shoulder and down his arm. "I'll try my best not to let that happen."

"We are lucky to have you at Thornbury," Rolf said, knowing now that his friend was in good hands.

"Nay," she said curtly. She stood up abruptly and looked up at Rolf, her expression serious. "I am not of the estate. I am from the forest. And you are lucky it was Lady Augusta who sent for me and my cousin Abby who came. I would not be here otherwise. I don't mix well with the manor folk, nor they with me."

"And why is that?" Rolf asked, surprised at her sudden surly demeanor.

"They are a loud and suspicious lot," she said without malice. "Most of them know little of healing, except what they see of the barber. And what they don't know, they don't like."

"Are you saying you have been persecuted in Thornbury for your practices?"

"I didn't stay around long enough to let them, my lord. Do you know about my family, about Millicent and my parents?"

"No, nothing," he answered.

"Well, one day, you ask your lady, and she'll tell you. I find it easier to live in the forest, where people keep to themselves. They know they can count on me for help if they need it. In return, there are no whisperings about 'witchery.'"

"I had a feeling it was that." For an instant, Rolf felt guilty, having had a moment's thought about her as a witch, himself. However, now that he'd spoken with her, he thought her merely unusual. She had nothing of the enchanter about her.

"Why do you come at Augusta's bidding, if no one else's at the manor?"

Her face lit up in a particularly warm smile. "Again, you ask your lady about that someday. And know that in my regard for Lady Augusta, I'm not so unusual. You'll find most of the people in Thornbury, and even farther afield, either owe her a debt of gratitude or have a great fondness for her. She has her own special brand of healing you'll discover. That is," and here she paused and fixed him with a penetrating gaze, "if you care enough to find out."

He hesitated just an instant, startled at the personal turn their conversation had taken. With her intense stare, her brow creased in concentration, she seemed to be taking his measure.

"I assure you, Bernadine of the forest, that I intend to discover all there is to know about my lady and make her as happy as she has apparently made all those around her."

He was rewarded with another smile, albeit a wry one.

Impulsively, he reached out a hand and touched her forearm. She flinched slightly but did not pull away.

"Know too that I am grateful you came for my friend's sake. He is like a brother to me."

Bernadine nodded.

THIS WAS HOW AUGUSTA found them, standing closely together with her betrothed's hand on the healer's arm, with them seemingly looking deeply into each other's eyes.

A hot rush of jealousy like she had never experienced before slammed through her. It struck her so strongly she nearly dropped the broth pot she'd intercepted from one of the servants.

Rolf's hand only days earlier had disgusted her with his dirty nails, yet she had come to think of him as her own, especially since he'd bathed and tied his hair back.

Was her betrothed attracted to this woman? And who could blame him, she thought, if he was. Wasn't Bernadine equally as beautiful as Millie? And were both sisters not completely opposite to herself, with their fair hair and graceful ways? Augusta suddenly felt like an ungainly clod.

Hearing her entrance, she watched them both turn to her at once. Rolf dropped his hand, not quickly but casually.

"How . . . how is Perry?" Augusta asked when she found her voice.

Perhaps Bernadine saw something in her lady's face, but she quickly came forward to take the kettle.

"He will be better if he has less people coming in every five minutes asking how he is," she said with some gruffness as she hung the iron pot over the fire to keep it hot.

"Then I'll go," Rolf said, "but keep me informed if anything changes."

"Aye, that I will," she said. "Now take her ladyship out and begin to make those discoveries you vowed," she added, literally pushing them with a hand on each of their backs toward the hall.

When the wooden door closed firmly in their faces, Rolf and Augusta looked at each other awkwardly for a moment.

"*Hm,*" Rolf said. "She seems quite a capable . . . and exceptional woman."

Augusta nodded and turned not toward the solar but away from it, with her dog at her heel. Down the stairs and out the side door, she walked out into the evening coolness. When she realized that Rolf was still beside her, she added, "Yes, and quite beautiful don't you think?"

"Well, yes," he answered without thinking, "just like her sister."

Augusta winced. If only he'd said, just like you, she would have forgiven the lie in the face of its sweetness. She stiffened her back, vowing that it didn't matter how he viewed her as long as he saved Thornbury for her family and gave her an heir.

She walked through the open garden gate and nearly closed it in his face. As it was, the huge oak portal caught him in the shoulder.

"*Ow!*" he exclaimed. "What on earth . . .?"

"Did I hurt you?" Augusta asked, sauntering over to the cold stone bench. "Perhaps you should hurry back to Bernadine so she can tend to you."

"'Tis not serious," he told her.

The dog put his nose and front paws up on her lap, clearly noticing his mistress's mood. She rewarded him with a good scratch on top of his head and behind his floppy ears.

"I love you, Rolf," she murmured.

The words seemed to hang in the still night air. As if Augusta only just heard them herself, she looked chagrined over her dog's head at her betrothed. It annoyed her to have said those words in his presence even though they were directed merely at her hound.

Rolf had a slightly shocked look on his face, she realized. *As if the concept of love between them had never entered his mind.* That irked her even more. *By Jove's teeth!* Why was the stuff of man and woman so damnably confusing? She glared at him.

"What is the matter with you?" he asked, still massaging his shoulder with his hand as he sat beside her on the bench.

"*Grr,*" growled Rolf, the dog.

"Nothing is the matter with me," she continued to stroke the dog's head. "And what did Bernadine mean about 'the discoveries you vowed'?"

Rolf sighed, clearly baffled by her behavior.

HE LOOKED UP AT the sky. How to begin to discover the lady beside him, he knew not. He had always bedded a woman, barely speaking to her, not caring about the thoughts in her head or the emotions of her heart. At present, he did indeed want to discover what made Gus happy and how she managed to make those around her so content as well.

"Look at the moon, it is quite blue tonight," Rolf commented.

"*Mm,* like Bernadine's eyes," she said back.

Nay, that wasn't what he'd been thinking at all.

"And the stars are so bright," he added when she was silent again.

"You mean like Bernadine's hair? Or Millie's?"

"Nay, I——" he stopped short as it dawned on him. What an oaf! His own words came back to him: *capable, exceptional,* beautiful?

Yes, like her sister.

"Are you jealous of Bernadine?" he asked, his eyes widening in disbelief.

She looked anywhere but at him, until he took her chin between his thumb and finger and turned her face toward his own.

"Grr," growled Rolf again.

He ignored the hound, even at the risk of being bitten, until Gus wrenched her chin free of his grasp and pushed the dog's paws and head off her lap at the same time.

She narrowed her eyes and pursed her lips, looking as though she wanted to squash him as one flattens midges on a midsummer night.

"Of course not," she said, straightening her gown where Rolf had crumpled it. "But I don't know you that well, not your character, anyway. I wouldn't want to see you compromise a young woman whom I've personally summoned to Thornbury. She is under my protection."

"Compromise a young . . . ," he repeated. Perhaps he had mistaken her earlier comments. Perhaps she was not jealous, but merely did not trust him.

"I assure you that I am not about to pounce on every woman who enters the house, not while my friend lies wounded and in that woman's care," he added.

"Scoundrel," she said, clearly not liking his answer at all. "What about *after* Perry is well? Then will you pounce?"

"Then we'll be married," he reminded her.

"And then I suppose you'll have eyes only for me?"

He hated to lie to her, though it sounded as if she needed a little shoring up when it came to self-confidence. For answer, he stood up and reached out his hand, waiting patiently until she deigned to lay hers on his. Then he drew her up to stand beside him.

"Close your mouth," he ordered the dog as it once more began to growl.

To Augusta's surprise, Rolf did, laying his head back down on her shoe.

"And you, my lady, open yours."

Dumbfounded, she did so, if only to gasp at his words. However, as she did, he bent his head to kiss her. She closed her eyes, waiting with her lips parted.

He paused, staring at her sweet face. A second later, her eyelids fluttered open, confusion in the depths of her warm brown gaze. He was but inches from her.

"I am sorry about your shoulder, I—" she began.

He silenced her with a touch of his finger to her lips. "Gus, let me breathe you, let me taste you."

Her eyes opened wider, and he slipped his hands onto her shoulders, then down her back, holding her safely against him. He knew he was embracing her tightly, but if she could barely breathe, perhaps she would be quiet and listen.

"Before going into battle, I used to find out everything I could about my enemy. I would study them because then I would know their weaknesses and—"

"You seek to learn how I am weak?" she interrupted.

He couldn't help sighing. "No," he drew his finger up her exposed neck to her gently rounded chin. Then he halted at her tanned cheek.

"I would know your strengths, Gus. Your weaknesses you'll show me when you are ready to trust me. Only when I knew my enemies' strengths, then was I prepared to fight them, or in your case, to commit myself. Your strengths I would learn now."

He placed a hand on either side of her startled face and while holding her still, finally brought his lips to hers.

HIS KISS WAS GENTLE at first, yet still, it knocked all the air out of her lungs with its power. She felt the pressure of his firm lips increase upon her own, and realized that he tilted his head slightly so that his mouth slanted against hers. Her eyes had somehow drifted closed again, and quickly, she opened them to see his looking back at her. Then he raised his head.

"I would know you, Gus, all of you."

Augusta was breathing hard. *Her first kiss, her first kiss!* Yet all she could say was, "When we are married, it will be your right and my duty."

He broke away abruptly, sighing with exasperation. Instantly the night air whisked around her, and she wrapped her arms around herself to ward it off. She had offended him, and in return he had stopped the pleasure of that wonderful kiss. He was offering her a gift and she'd thrown it back at him with talk of rights and duty.

She was clumsy in the ways of this way as in all others. Reaching her hand out to him, she touched the same shoulder she'd banged with the gate.

HE LOOKED DOWN AT her hand then back at her.

"Rights be damned," he said, keeping his tone low and gentle. Still, she dropped her hand from him as if scalded.

"You are being intentionally difficult," he continued. "I'm not talking about lawful duties but about wants and desires. And trust. Do you trust me?"

"I trust that you'll marry me and try to beget an heir."

"Yes, that I will."

He thought again about Bernadine's words. He could not let Gus retire for the evening yet, not without speaking with her further. Not when that simple kiss had sent desire right through him to the soles of his feet.

"Are you cold?"

"Yes."

He took her hand in his and wordlessly led her back to the house. They couldn't expect any degree of privacy downstairs, so he climbed the stairs and went directly to the king's solar, passing by the suite of rooms given over to Wesley and his family.

The thought of Wesley residing so close by irked Rolf, even as he pushed the door open to find Lord Brenville already there, sharing a toddy with Montmorency.

"Join us, young Rolf," came Brenville's voice.

"Another time," he said curtly and backed out.

He looked down at Gus, who shrugged.

"To your chamber then," he decided and led her there before she could protest.

With satisfaction, he closed the door in the face of the drooling dog and scanned the chamber. The drapes were drawn, the fire lit, and a small carafe of wine sat upon the bureau, but thankfully, Millie was nowhere to be seen.

Gus had a sitting area next to the windows, and there they sat facing each other. In the silence, as he took in her room's interior for the first time, noting her large bed with the fine hangings, he thought of the kiss and wondered if it mattered whether they waited to fornicate until after the wedding.

Then perhaps due to nervousness, he said utterly the wrong thing and knew he had done so as soon as he uttered the words, "Bernadine told me I should ask you about her family."

He watched Gus stiffen, then reach down automatically to pat her ever-present hound. When her hand felt nothing but air, she sat back up, looking utterly lost.

What a dimwit, he was. Naturally his bride was jealous of the effortlessly beautiful Bernadine. He would have to work harder to make her understand that he had absolutely no intentions of risking their marriage over a dalliance with the healer or anyone else.

"What do you want to know about Bernadine?" she asked, her voice almost a whisper. At the same time, she reached over to pour herself a drink.

"Madeira?" she offered him though there was only one glass, which she came perilously close to knocking over.

He shook his head. "Thank you, no. And there's really nothing I want to know about Bernadine. She said that *you* were the reason she came to help Perry. That's what I want to know about."

"Oh, that," she shrugged, taking a sip. "Some time ago, I helped her family. Her mother, Alesandre, was a healer, too, and she tended to my own mother on her deathbed. Some of the people hereabouts who loved my mother wanted to blame Alesandre. I wouldn't let them harass her. It doesn't matter now though. Bernadine and Millie's parents have moved back to France. I kept Millie on as my maid, and, as you know, Bernadine chooses to live almost in isolation."

She shifted her legs, curling them under her and adjusting her skirts. "She inherited the healing arts from her mother and also the suspicions of the good people of Thornbury, I'm afraid. But I won't hear anyone speak ill of her. We had a bit of a witch hunt here a few years back and I put a stop to it. That's all nonsense."

Rolf guessed that there may have been a bit more to Gus's aid than she cared to go into. Certainly, she'd won the loyalty of the two sisters and, at the same time, managed to keep the affection of her people.

"You must be something of a diplomat, my lady."

She shrugged again. "I use common sense that sometimes people lose when they let their emotions get in the way."

"And what about *your* emotions, Gus? Don't you ever let them run wild?"

She blushed to the roots of her hair. "Why, I don't know."

Before he changed his mind, Rolfe knelt down on the floor in front of her, happy not to share the space with the hound. "I want to kiss you again. May I?"

She couldn't look him in the eye. "You don't have to ask?"

"Why? Because it's my *right* to kiss you?" He held her chin so she had to meet his gaze.

"No," she replied, her voice husky to his ears, "because I want you to."

He swallowed, watching as the dark pupils of her eyes seemed to pulse with her heartbeat. Then he put his hands in her hair behind her head and pulled her forward to meet him. When the half-full glass of Madeira crashed down, spilling over her lap and over his trousers, he ignored it.

She parted her lips expectantly this time, and he kissed her, finding the taste of her sweet as before and mixed with the flavor of the wine. She was like no one he'd ever kissed before.

He realized then that he hadn't kissed that many women, not on the mouth anyway. The kind of dalliances he'd had with nameless women whose faces he barely saw at the time and certainly could not now remember were the type where kissing was not desired, nor desirable. Sadly, those women were little more than spread legs or a skilled mouth to satisfy him, women who made their living servicing naval officers and did so for a fair penny.

With Gus, he couldn't tear himself away from her warm lips. He deepened the kiss, slipping his tongue inside her mouth. And as if with a will of its own, his hand was suddenly sliding up her rib cage and cupping her full breast.

Hearing Gus moan and feeling her body relax into him, it nearly did him in. He brushed his thumb up and over her nipple, and knew that he had to follow with his mouth. He wanted to take her right then in her bed chamber and damn the formalities of the church.

He paused a moment, thinking of their earlier encounters.

"Where's Millie?"

"What?" Gus looked so befuddled for a moment, he couldn't help kissing her again, this time he lingered along her chin line to her right ear and nibbled on her lobe.

"Is she going to come barging in here?" he asked between bites.

"No," Gus said. "I gave her the afternoon and evening off before I knew that we'd need her sister's services. She'll be with her young man, Jared."

"Good."

Rolf pulled her down to join him on the soft wool rug. When she was under him, he pushed down the fabric of her bodice so he could take one pink, delightfully thrusting nipple into his mouth.

"Rolf," she breathed out his name at the same time gripping his shoulders with fierce tight fingers.

In response, he rubbed his teeth against her taut pink nub, teasing and tasting, sucking and gently biting. He was mildly shocked when she grasped at his hair, tugging his head so he could lavish the same attention on her other breast, which she arched toward his mouth.

Thank God, his future wife was no prude. Just inexperienced. And waiting for him to give her every new experience he could think of. He could feel all of her body arching toward him and his own was straining against her, grinding his pelvis into the soft, warm place between her legs.

Jesus, how had they gone from the cold stone bench in the garden to this so quickly? He lifted his head to look down at Gus's flushed face. She was incredibly beautiful that night. Her eyes were sparkling like firelit brandy, her cheeks were flushed, her lips were ruddy and moistened by her own Madeira-sweetened tongue, even then darting out to lick them.

How had he ever thought her hair plain? Spread out around her pretty face, it was picking up every warm amber color from the fireplace—roan browns with streaks of red and gold and honeyed amber.

Moreover, she was all his. He lowered his head to kiss her once again.

"Fire," she said urgently against his mouth, her body suddenly stiff under his.

Yes, he thought, they were both practically on fire with wanting.

"Rolf, fire," she repeated, pushing at his chest. "Outside."

Her words finally penetrated to his lust-filled brain, and he turned to follow where her gaze led. The unmistakable dancing of flames, somewhere down below, reflected orange and red upon the panes of glass.

"Bloody hell," he exclaimed, feeling a painful ache in his groin as he got up quickly and went to the window. She was beside him in an instant, fidgeting with her clothes at the same time that she scanned the courtyard.

"Something's ablaze near the stables," he said. "Stay here," he yelled over his shoulder as he ran to the door. When he opened it, her dog streaked past him into the room, and Rolf charged down the hallway, praying that there was no loss of life, man nor horse.

CHAPTER SIX

"**S**tay here!" she repeated, speaking to the empty doorway. Grabbing the Madeira carafe, she took a long draught to calm her racing heart and tumbling emotions before looking out the window once more.

Stay in her room while Thornbury burned? Impossible, she vowed, taking another swig while she watched servants spill out of the many doors, running hither and yon. Brenville is *my* home and I won't stand by idly.

Following in Rolf's footsteps, Augusta headed along the corridor, her panting hound beside her. She encountered her father and Walter coming out of the solar.

"What's all the ruckus?" the elder Brenville asked.

"A fire, Father, near the stables." And she ran past him down the stairs, feeling as if her head were swimming with the excitement of Rolf's kisses and caresses, and then the terror of the fire.

In the great hall, she found a swarm of servants, probably roused by Rolf's charging through and calling out an alarm. Even Wesley and his entourage were there, some in their nightclothes, staying warm by the fire but remaining close to the exit should they need to flee the building. She didn't stop to talk.

Outside, she saw the stable boys already tossing buckets of sand and water on the blaze that seemed to have sprung to life in the hay barn. The head groom, as well as his staff and the groundskeepers, were also working to put out the blaze. David worked alongside Rolf to smother the flames with blankets. It appeared that they were winning, but she knew how treacherous a fire could be. They had lost their bakery twice in the past few years. She went as close as she dared without attracting Rolf's attention and called to the closest stable lad.

"Jeremy, get the horses out of there."

"The flames be almost out, milady."

"I don't care. I want those horses out in the open."

"Aye, milady." And the lad disappeared through the dark stable door beside the hay barn.

She waited a full minute, but when he didn't come back out, she thought of Rolf's huge destrier and decided Jeremy might need some help. She looked about yet saw no one who was not already occupied. She had hoped to find Wesley but couldn't see him anywhere in the midst of the chaos.

"Blast and bother!" she exclaimed, wiping her forehead, surprised to find herself moist. Think, she urged herself, but her head felt decidedly light, and though the night air was quite cool, her body was actually hot, perhaps sweating. Seeing no other choice, Augusta ran quickly toward the stables.

Inside, she paused. Where was the boy?

"Jeremy?" she called out.

The only answer was the alarmed whinnying of the horses who no doubt could smell the fire and were obviously fearful. Their hooves battered at their stall doors in a panic. She decided to forego leading them out in an orderly manner and unlatched the first stall door. She was nearly flattened as Perry's horse smashed the door open on its hinges and charged out.

Next, she worked to release two of her own horses though she was having increasing difficulty working the latches as her fingers felt like the bones were melting. Her father's and Rolf's horses were in the succeeding stalls.

However, as she reached out for another latch, two things caught her eye at once: a lick of flame high upon the back window which meant the fire must now be on the roof of the stables. Then, oddly, she saw a boy's foot, sticking out of the straw pile at the back of the stables beneath the very same window. No doubt a boy was attached.

Puzzled for a moment, she took a step toward the straw only to see Jeremy lying in a twisted heap.

"Oh, my God!" She was not the type to utter a piercing scream, but she had to summon help, and quickly.

"Rolf," was the first word out of her mouth, and her dog began to bark. The barn was beginning to spin around her and she had the urge simply to lie down.

"Rolf," she screamed again, louder this time, urgently, and something—most likely her dog—nearly knocked her off her feet. Suddenly, a strong grip went around her shoulders. For a second she felt utter relief. *Rolf!*

Yet in the next instant, terror raced through her foggy mind as a cloth soaked in some strong herb was clamped over her nose and mouth until she couldn't breathe. She couldn't turn her head to see who was there. Futilely, she clawed at the arm that held her, until all her strength melted from her body, and there was only blackness.

ROLF KNEW HE HAD heard Gus's voice. From where? The flames had been smothered in the hay barn, but there were so many people and horses milling about that he couldn't see her. He looked up to her bed chamber window where it seemed a long time ago, they shared a moment of pure passion, though in truth it had been less than fifteen minutes. However, she was not in the window calling down to him.

One of Gus's horses ran past him. Who had released the horses? He had given no orders for it. Just then, Peter called out, "More flames. On the stables roof."

Everyone surged in that direction. Some men climbed onto the roof while others passed up buckets of water. People from the town of Thornbury, it seemed, had rushed up the hill to help. Still, Rolf could not see Gus, but what he heard next made his blood run cold—her hound baying as loudly as he'd ever heard a dog bark.

Without hesitating, he ran into the stables. Garish orange light from the flames surged through the back window and the holes in the roof. As he hurried farther into the interior, that light was enough for him to see a stable boy, lying on the floor, much too close to the fire. He carried the boy outside into the waiting arms of Lord Brenville himself.

"Have you seen Augusta?" Rolf asked him.

"Yes, earlier. Outside the solar. She went rushing past like a badger on a scent after telling us there was a fire."

The dog barked again, clearly in distress.

Rolf charged back into the stables. He glanced into each empty stall he passed but headed for the sound of Gus's dog, barking and clawing against the gate that imprisoned it. Unlatching the half-door, Rolf stood back as her hound rushed out, but she was not there behind it.

The dog went directly to the next stall, baying madly. Rolf wrenched it open, relieved as his own courser cantered out of the building to safety. Then he saw Gus, lying prone against the back wall, her dog already running to stand next to her.

"Gus," he exclaimed, beside her in two strides and on his knees. For a moment, he feared her dead, so shallowly did she breathe. But even when he saw the rise and fall of her chest, his fear did not lessen. Had his own horse trampled her as she'd tried to release it from the stable? Even now were all her ribs broken beneath her sweetly soft skin?

Running his palms over her body, Rolf could find nothing amiss, not even a bump on her head. Quickly, he ran his hands over her arms and legs. She was whole, with no wound or injury that he could find, yet she was absolutely unconscious.

Rolf hated to move her in case he somehow hurt her more, but the fire still burned above them. As gently as he could, he lifted her into his arms and fled the stables.

When he emerged into the dark night, the first people who could see them exclaimed her name. Then others said it. He heard it over and over. "Lady Augusta!" "Lady Augusta!"

It filtered back to those who couldn't see what was happening, through everyone in the courtyard until a palpable hush descended over the entire crowd.

Everything seemed to freeze for the briefest of moments. Then Millie's shriek rent the night, as she came running into the courtyard from the direction of the kitchens with a young man Rolf had never seen before.

"Oh, milady," she exclaimed.

Her terror galvanized the crowd into action once again. Suddenly, Rolf was overwhelmed with people offering to help carry her, to fetch her some water. *What was wrong with her? Where had he found her?* He had to push past the tide of concerned folk all talking at once.

"Millie," he called over the noise of the crowd and the dog, "help me get her inside so your sister can tend her."

"My sister?" the young woman repeated, and he realized she hadn't known that Bernadine had been brought to the manor. Yet without further question, she did her best to help clear a path, shouting at people to move aside, and then ran in front of him up the stairs to turn down the bedding in her lady's chamber.

Rolf stood in the middle of the room, not wanting to put Gus down. Instead, he gripped her more tightly as the dog circled his feet.

"Go get Bernadine," he told Millie. "She is in the lieutenant's chamber. He was wounded today."

The young woman hesitated with her hand over her mouth, staring at her mistress who drooped unmoving in Rolf's arms.

"Now!" he ordered.

Millie turned and ran out of the room.

Approaching the bed, he laid the lady of the manor carefully upon her sheets and then pulled her blanket and counterpane over her.

She was as still as . . . He couldn't finish the thought. Leaning close, he brushed his lips against her forehead and breathed her scent in.

"Come on, Gus. Wake up." He brushed his hand over her pale cheek. Pale! He'd never seen her pale before, and he realized how much he liked her sun-kissed skin. It always made her appear as if she were in a flush of activity, which she usually was.

He stroked her hair. "I can't take this twice in one day. First Perry and now you. There is a wedding to which we must both attend, and I'll not let you back out on me now."

Just then, he heard footsteps approaching and sat up. Bernadine came running into the room along with Lord Brenville, followed by Millie.

"What happened?" her father spoke first, coming to stand at the foot of his daughter's bed.

Without waiting for an answer, Bernadine climbed onto the bed and knelt down, placing her hands on Augusta's cheeks.

Rolf hated that he had so little information. "I don't know. I found her in the stables, but I can't see anything wrong with her. Not even a small bump to her head."

He stood helplessly and watched while Bernadine opened each of Augusta's eyelids gently, then let them fall back into place. Then she lay her ear against her chest, listening to the rhythm of her heartbeat. Whatever she heard caused her to gasp softly.

Clearly puzzled, she sat back a moment and considered.

"Well?" he asked, hearing the strain in his own voice.

But she didn't answer at first. Suddenly, she put her face very close to Augusta's and sniffed. Rolf thought he saw her jump. Then she opened Augusta's mouth and sniffed again.

"God in heaven!" she muttered. Then she turned to her sister.

"Millie, quick. Run as fast as you can to the cook. Get some hyssop and bring boiling water with it. Every moment you delay could mean your lady's life."

Rolf couldn't stifle an oath born of fear.

"Good God," exclaimed Lord Brenville, gripping one of the bed posts and looking as though he might swoon.

Millie had already disappeared in haste.

"What's wrong with her?" Rolf asked, feeling as if he couldn't get enough air into his lungs.

"Poisoned," Bernadine said succinctly. "White opium poppy to be exact. First a tincture held over her mouth and nose to render her unconscious, then someone must have dripped it into her mouth, for she has to have ingested it, so greatly is she affected. It is as though she drank a draught of it."

Rolf shook his head. "How can this be? I was with her . . .," he trailed off, thinking of their last moments, rolling around on this very floor, "then the fire. She was only out of my sight for a few minutes. She must have gone to the stables to help out."

Millie came running in then, along with cook and half the kitchen staff. In her hands, she held a canister of hedge hyssop that had already been dried and powdered. The cook held out a black pot of scalding hot water.

"Just boiled," she said, eyeing her motionless mistress. "For late night tea," she added, setting it down on the trivet by the fire. "Is she . . .?"

"Everyone out," Rolf ordered the other servants while Bernadine and Millie went to work. As the kitchen servants left, the sisters mixed a small amount of the ground hyssop powder with the boiling water, and when it was cool enough, they forced the liquid down Augusta's throat, teaspoon full by teaspoon full.

Then they waited in silence except for Millie's stifled crying. Bernadine busied herself removing Augusta's shoes and rubbing her feet, hands, and legs.

"They're getting cold," she explained to Rolf who stood grimly beside the bed. "Help me, start rubbing her."

He did as he was told. Placing his large hands upon Gus's cool, smooth skin, he rubbed and kneaded her right arm and hand. Then he moved to her stocking-clad leg, mirroring Bernadine's actions, not even worrying about the impropriety of his hands under his betrothed skirts, yet feeling as if their actions were pointless.

Gus seemed already quite lifeless. He was losing someone whom he was only just beginning to realize could be as precious to him as his own life. He watched her father begin to rub her feet, gingerly at first, then with vigor. Rolf's eyes raised to the face of the man who should become his father-in-law. There were tears in the elder Brenville's eyes.

For a moment, the two men locked glances. Rolf felt something pass unspoken between them, perhaps just a kinship of feeling for this remarkably competent woman.

"What will happen now?" Rolf asked at last, when Bernadine checked her for signs of life again.

"The poison draws the blood from ones' extremities, while it slowly sends one deeper and deeper into sleep. Eventually, her heart will stop beating unless the purgative reaches her stomach in time to stop much more of the poison going into her system. The hyssop should cause her to vomit. If it doesn't, then she'll die."

He had been looking at Gus's peaceful face until Bernadine uttered that last word. His gaze fixed on the blond healer then, who appeared emotionless and so stoic.

"You say that as if there is nothing else you can do."

"There isn't." She gave a bitter twist to her lips. "Contrary to what some folk say, I'm no witch and I have no magic to bring the lady back. But I swear if I did, I would use it. There's nothing worse than the waiting."

Rolf realized then that she wasn't emotionless, just experienced in these matters as any seasoned soldier, enough to know that there was nothing gained by hysterics. She was a most unusual female—as was Gus.

"Right now, I wish you were a witch," Millie chimed in, "if only she would awaken."

"She'll come back to us," Lord Brenville said, his voice sounding deep and scratchy, thick with emotion.

"She's been through a lot, haven't you, my girl?" he added, giving Augusta's leg a pat. "Kept us all safe last time the ague reached us. Not a death in Thornbury. And you increased the profits from the honey and jam sales to Bristol. Remember when you first learned to read, dearest, you climbed up on my lap and said everything was going to be all right, for you could handle the books then. And you were right, Augusta, you've done it all for so many years. Even though I haven't made it easy. In fact, I've been a damned fool."

The tears were rolling down the old man's face now, his eyes seeing only the face of his daughter.

Rolf looked at Gus's face, as her father added, "Brenville can't survive without you."

Just then, Gus started to cough. It started as a small sound in the back of her throat, then a splutter, then Bernadine was turning her on her side, holding her over the bucket that she had ready.

If Rolf felt helpless before, he felt downright useless now. All he could do was rub Gus's back as she vomited over and over, even when there was nothing left inside her, even when the heaving was dry and painful. Until at last, it was over and Bernadine let her patient recline once more upon her back. Still, Gus had not opened her eyes or spoken.

The room was silent as Bernadine wiped Augusta's lips and Millie stepped forward to smooth her lady's hair from her forehead. Rolf was aware that Gus's breathing had deepened. He reached a hand out to her at the same time that Bernadine did. Her skin was warmer to his touch. Or was it? He looked to the healer.

She looked back at him and nodded ever so slightly. "I think we caught it in time."

Millie placed her own hand on her lady's forehead. "To think, all this was going on while I was . . . was enjoying an afternoon off. I should never have left my mistress, not even for half a day."

An afternoon off. That's what Gus had said when he'd asked after Millie.

"Devil take him," he muttered. What an idiot he'd been. He glanced around Gus's chamber.

"Who prepared the room for her tonight?" he asked. "Who lit the fire?" He stood up suddenly and went over to the small seating area, looking until he found the cup. It was empty. He grabbed the carafe in his other hand. He sniffed it and then handed it to Bernadine who also breathed in the scent of what remained. She even dipped her finger in the dark liquid and placed a small drop on her tongue. She nodded, holding it out to him. Taking it back, he hurled its contents into the fire, which hissed and spat.

"Gus drank it while I was in the room with her. I let her be poisoned right in front of me," he admitted, feeling contempt for himself. He had assumed that Millie was responsible for preparing the chamber, and even when Gus told him otherwise, his lust-filled brain had not processed the information. If he were one of his own men, he'd have himself flogged for stupidity and negligence.

ROLF WAITED BY HER bedside all night. He couldn't say why exactly. After all, he didn't love the woman. Not yet. He'd known her such a short while. Yet their futures were tied together now, and with certainty he felt in his gut, he needed her as much as she needed him. Moreover, they would not only be about *her* estate and *his* money.

Looking at her placid face, with her mouth curved gently in sleep, something shifted inside him. Their marriage could be something much more.

As soon as Bernadine said she thought Gus would survive, Rolf had gotten rid of everyone. The healer gave him some instructions and went back to her vigil by Perry's bedside. Millie had gone downstairs to spread the news that their lady lived despite being poisoned. And Peter came to say that the fires were out and no person nor animal was injured save a young stable boy who had been hit on the head but was recovering.

After that, even Lord Brenville had finally been convinced to go to his chamber for some rest.

Rolf lifted his head from the pillow where he lay beside Gus. As he had done many times in the past hour, he just watched her, making sure her breath was still steady. She looked as he imagined she would when she was in normal sleep. But he couldn't say for sure as he'd never slept with her. He stroked her cheek, which had more of its usual color in it. How odd that this would be their first night together, both of them fully dressed and her unconscious. Would she be angry if she knew of the impropriety taking place? He thought not.

Just then, there was a rap on the door. Bone weary, Rolf rolled out of bed and opened the door. It was Wesley.

"You," Rolf ground out. He had to restrain himself from popping the man a fast and hard fist into his face. If he found even the smallest shred of proof that Wesley was responsible for any of this, he'd run him through with his sword and then shoot him with his pistol.

"Uh, yes," Wesley looked disconcerted to see Rolf. "I was expecting the maid or . . . uh . . . that is . . ."

"Lady Brenville is *my* bride. Naturally, I will stay here by her side and protect her after someone has tried to kill her."

"Yes, of course. How is she?"

Rolf could barely answer the man. "She lives."

"I couldn't sleep for worrying about my cousin," Wesley went on, as if oblivious to Rolf's hostility. "And the wedding?"

"What about it?" Rolf asked through clenched teeth.

"Naturally, I wondered if I should send word to my brother and his wife. That is, if it were postponed."

"It will go on as planned," Rolf said, though in the back of his mind, he began to doubt it. After all, his best man lay wounded, his bride was still unconscious. He couldn't stand at the altar alone. That was assuming he was still standing by the day of the wedding.

"Is there anything else?" Rolf asked.

"Just tell Augusta that I—"

Rolf closed the door in his face. He remained there a moment, listening for the man's footsteps to depart. Instead, he heard another pair arrive. *God's wounds!* His patience was being tried.

Yanking the door open with a vengeance, he was surprised to see a stranger.

"I'm the surgeon from Bristol," said the short man with gray hair.

Rolf sighed. "You are no longer needed. I'm sure someone in the kitchen will give you a good meal for your trouble."

The man bristled. "I am paid in good coin, sir."

"When you do good work, no doubt." Rolf looked past the surgeon to where Wesley still stood. "Will you take this man to Lieutenant Peregrine Newbury's chamber and see if the healer has use of him there? Leave the decision to her."

"I will," Wesley said, surprising Rolf with his compliance.

When they disappeared, he closed the door again. Still leaning against it, he was contemplating their shaky future when Gus murmured something. Rolf was beside her in an instant.

"Gus," he said softly, taking hold of her hand.

"Iyetbigick," she mumbled.

He stroked his thumb across the back of her hand, relief washing over him.

"I don't know what you're saying," he told her. "Can you open your eyes?"

Nothing happened for a moment, and he thought she'd gone back to sleep. Then, as if her eyelids were far too heavy for her, she opened her eyes very slowly. At first, she focused on the canopy above her, and then ever so gradually, she turned her eyes toward him without moving her head. Rolf noticed that her gaze was clear with not a hint of the insanity that sometimes followed unconsciousness.

"Ihatebeingsick," she said, and this time he understood her words that all ran together.

He actually laughed. "I imagine you would. It's hard to boss everyone around while you're flat on your back."

"Not bossy," she countered, and this time, she turned her head toward him, only to wince. "What happened?" she asked, struggling to raise a hand to her head. He imagined that it throbbed rather badly.

"You were poisoned," he told her flatly, seeing no reason to lie to her.

He watched her eyes widen with alarm and fear. Then she closed them, and everything that was her seemed to disappear with the shutting of her warm brown eyes. He felt a moment of loss—long enough to foretell how it would be to live at Thornbury if she were not there. He realized that it would be intolerable

"Am I dying?" she asked at last.

"No," Rolf assured her immediately. Though she might have done, and that thought drained him. In fact, he was bloody exhausted. Rather than taking a few steps to walk around her bed, he climbed over her, feeling her body tense before he lay down heavily on the other side of her bed, resting his head on the empty pillow. He knew he smelled of smoke and fire and fear, but she'd have to live with him not bathing that night.

Everything was still for a moment. Then, to his astonishment, Gus rolled onto her side and put her hand on his chest. Her eyes were still closed, but she scooted closer and managed to rest her head on his arm. It was uncomfortable as hell, but he didn't care. He caressed her shoulder and arm with his free hand and then pulled the coverlet over both of them as best he could.

This was just how married people must comfort each other, he thought.

As if reading his mind, she murmured, "So we shall be married after all."

Damn right they would. Come hell or high water! He squeezed her closer against him, ignoring the numbing in his arm where her head rested. All the hounds of hell were not going to stop them. And certainly not some cowardly assassin, be it Wesley or someone else!

CHAPTER SEVEN

By the time Augusta was allowed out of her chamber, two days later, all the rest of the guests had arrived. Even Lloyd, fresh from purchasing horses, and James with his wife, Helen, along with her retinue, had arrived after the midday meal.

"Is James the paragon of virtue that Wesley is?" Rolf asked Gus as they stood in the dining room by the carefully laid table, awaiting Lord Brenville and the rest of the guests. He held her elbow, though she'd assured him that she could stand quite well by herself.

She shrugged off his snide remark as she did all his passing quips about Wesley. He looked at her, still paler than usual, but otherwise, none the worse for her ordeal.

"I still say that it's not Wesley or James you should be worrying about," she said, watching with alarm as the servants brought in the first course of pigeons in white sauce, placing the dishes carefully on the sideboard. About ten minutes too early!

Rolf took a deep, steadying breath. The timing was off on this normally well-run ship, ever since Gus was felled by the opium poppies.

"Do tell me precisely why I should not be worrying about your cousins." He loved to hear her theories regarding the poisoning and the archer.

"Well, James wasn't even around, and, Wesley, he's never been good with a bow though we played at archery for a summer. The pistol is more his weapon."

He rolled his eyes. "Where there is money involved, dear heart, there is a way."

At that moment, Wesley entered the room. Behind him came the man who must be his younger brother with the same features and fair hair. He led his lovely raven-haired wife, blooming with good health and obviously expecting.

"I don't believe you've been formally introduced to my king," Wesley said. "Captain, this is my brother, James."

Before Rolf could say anything, James stepped up—a trimmer version of Wesley—and saluted smartly. "You are a naval officer, are you not, my lord?"

Rolf nodded, seeing admiration in the younger man's face.

"Why, yes. I—"

"Were you at Trafalgar?" James asked.

In an instant, Rolf was transported back to that terrible day, the loss of life including Nelson, the smell of the cannons and the pistols, and the watery grave that claimed so many even in the face of English victory.

"Yes," he answered. *And Malta. And Boulogne. And . .*

.

"I am honored that we will even in a small manner be related," James continued. "I would like to have gone to sea."

Rolf wondered if he had an abnormality or injury or unapparent disfigurement, but the young man only sighed without enlightening him further.

"May I present my wife, Helen. Helen, this is Augusta's betrothed."

The lovely woman curtsied deeply despite her condition.

Rolf nodded in return, realizing belatedly that he should have taken her hand and kissed it. However, as Gus had learned, he was not fluent in the social graces.

Wesley, on the other hand, took Augusta's hand in both of his and held it captive, looking into her eyes.

"You look well, Coz," Wesley said, before turning to Rolf. "Clearly, you are taking excellent care of her."

Rolfe had to give the man credit for continuing to act as if he were a welcome guest and Rolf, the gracious host. For the ladies' sakes, he could play along, at least for the moment.

"We're happy to say Lady Augusta is recovering well so that none of you need be disappointed in your desire to attend a wedding." Rolf hoped that was the correct thing to say. As soon as he was forced to act as lord of the manor, he felt out of his realm.

In another moment, Gus took over, expressing concern over James' and Helen's long journey, exclaiming enthusiastically over Helen's dress and her hair as well as her obvious good health.

Watching them silently for a moment, Rolf noted James's wife's pretty face and attentive expression. She seemed a pleasant enough woman. Probably someone who also appreciated the sweet and clean Wesley, though she had James.

Similar in looks to his older brother, with the same pale hair, James seemed to have his hands full. He had a couple children at home and another on the way, not to mention guarding a lovely wife.

"Your engagement seems extremely fortuitous," Helen said, speaking to both Augusta and Rolf, but then placing a hand on his arm and adding, "Your career and your favorable ties to King George do you credit, my lord. I think you are an impressive addition to the family, and we welcome you."

"It appeared recently as if there would be more subtractions to this family than additions," Rolf said, just as Lord Brenville entered the room, gesturing for the Brenville clan and guests to take their seats.

"Yes, we heard," James said, seated across from Augusta. "Are you quite all right?"

"Perfectly fine," Augusta confirmed, clearly wanting to put an end to any discussion of her own health. "However, we heard that your lovely wife was unwell, at least temporarily."

"Much better now, aren't you, my dear?" James confirmed with Helen, next to him. She nodded and leaned close to say something into her husband's ear.

Rolf took the opportunity to lean close to Gus.

"You look lovely tonight, and much more like your former self." Her color was good, and the errant curl escaping the pins reminded him of how she looked when he first saw her.

Gus hated talking about her mishap. He noticed how she always deflected any comments to someone else's troubles.

True to form, she asked, "How is Perry? I half expected him to dine with us by this evening."

Not wanting to speak of his friend in front of the cousins, Rolf dismissed her question with a shrug, waiting until her father had seated himself and greeted everyone. Then as the wine was poured, he added, "He grows stronger daily and was asking to see you."

"Does he know about the fire and . . . about—?"

"Someone trying to kill you?" Rolf watched her wince. "Yes, he knows."

"What does he think?" she asked, taking a sip of wine.

"He agrees with me. If you had followed my orders, you would have been safer. That poor boy wouldn't have a lump on his head because someone wanted to get you into the stables, and you wouldn't have nearly been suffocated."

Belatedly, he realized his own annoyance at her disobedience had caused him to speak more loudly than he'd intended, and with a sharper tone.

She opened her mouth, but nothing came out. Instead, she pressed her lips into a firm line. Next, she lay her fork down while a flush spread over her face. Clearly, she was seething.

He nearly rolled his eyes. Though he had not meant to blurt out what had been on his mind since the night she'd directly disobeyed him and thrown herself into harm's way, now that he had, he meant to make her see the truth.

"You don't know that I would have been any safer if I'd stayed put," she said at last.

"Surely you are jesting," Rolf said, unable to keep the incredulity from his tone. "Without doubt, you would have been safer in your chamber than running into a burning stable. What nonsense are you saying?"

"But it was not the fire that got me, was it? If I'd stayed in my room, sipping my poisoned wine and fretting, like as not I'd be dead by the time anyone discovered me. *Rolf* saved my life, did he not?"

Devil take him, but she was right about that. What's more, the way she purposefully said the hound's name was an insinuation that he, her betrothed, had been remiss. It was his turn to go quiet for a moment, pressing his own lips together in annoyance.

"Nevertheless," Rolf said at last, "from now on, you will follow my orders exactly."

She paused, staring straight into his flinty gaze. "Until after the threat has passed, you mean?"

He laughed shortly. "By then you will be my wife," he told her as if speaking to a child. "Naturally, you'll follow my orders *after* the wedding."

She shook her head as if she hadn't heard correctly.

"Yes, I will be your wife, but not one of your men. I have lived a long time without a man telling me what to do—"

"And you have done quite nicely," he interrupted, intending a sincere compliment.

She narrowed her eyes, perhaps wondering if he were being condescending. He wasn't.

"I want this wedding, Rolf, but understand me, I won't become yours to command. Not now, not ever."

He sipped his wine and watched as the cold pigeon was placed before him, aware that at the quiet table, every word they said was being overheard. However, Gus was really off the mark now, and he needed to set her straight.

"The natural order of things," he began, and then found himself talking to her back.

She had stood up and, after mumbling an excuse to the room in general about still not feeling well, had walked away without even a backward glance.

Without even a trip or a stumble either, he noted. Her faithful hound, which must have been loitering under the table, followed along behind, and for that, Rolf was immensely grateful.

Taking a sip of his wine, which suddenly tasted like vinegar, he tried to offer a placid smile to the other diners while ignoring the interested glances of Helen and the cousins. They'd witnessed Gus walking off in a huff, but Rolf refused to look ruffled. He feared, however, that his smile looked as though he were baring his teeth.

Nevertheless, it was good that they had conducted a very necessary discussion and clarified their positions. If she thought he was going to become her husband in name only and follow her around like the other Rolf, she was sorely mistaken.

Moreover, if they'd been already married, he thought, taking a larger sip of the infernal wine, he would go upstairs right then and make her regret walking out on him. Not with his fists, as he knew some men did. No, never that! Yet he could think of many pleasant ways to make a woman beg for forgiveness and for other things.

Sighing, he gave up trying to keep a happy expression. It was going to be quite an ordeal bringing his bride to heel, but he would be damned if he'd become merely Lady Brenville's consort. He meant to become Lord of Thornbury in deed as well as in name, and he needed Gus's full support for that.

AUGUSTA DIDN'T KNOW WHEN she'd been so furious. Their conversation had started out innocently, too. What was the man thinking? She had run a successful, albeit impoverished estate for years. Who was Rolf to tell her that she would follow his orders? She slowed her pace on the stairs.

Who was he indeed? He was the man who would be her husband, who, with every legal right, could do with her as he wished. She leant against the stone wall, trying not to panic. Yet she knew so little of what type of orders he would issue. She knew so little about him. Then she heard the footsteps and couldn't help a heavy sigh.

"Millie," she said, turning to see her maid creeping along behind her. "It's bad enough that Rolf," she indicated the dog, "nearly trips me up everywhere I go. It was worse when Perry stuck to me like tar—though I might be dead if he hadn't. But having you suddenly following my every move . . ."

She broke off as Millicent's eyes welled up with tears.

"You were that close to being dead, milady."

They'd been through this about a dozen times already. All Augusta could do was wait for Millie to get a hold of herself.

"If it makes you feel better, you may come with me. Just stop skulking about."

Millie wiped her eyes on a piece of her skirt. "I never skulk," she muttered.

"Come on, then." Augusta continued up the stairs and found herself pausing at the landing. The lieutenant knew Rolf better than anyone. Yet would he tell her what she needed to know? She could but try, she thought, turning toward the end of the hall where Perry still recuperated.

"Milady?" Millie asked, quickening her step so she was beside Augusta.

"I don't suppose you'd go prepare my room for me and leave me in peace."

Millicent shook her head.

"Very well then. Wait right here."

She knocked softly on Perry's door, pushing it open when she heard Bernadine's voice.

In the low light of the candles, Augusta saw Bernadine sitting on Perry's bed, feeding him soup. Perry, for his part, looked so much better that Augusta couldn't help a broad smile. He returned it when he caught sight of her.

"Lady, I'm glad to see you up and around."

"It appears I have recovered more quickly than you," she teased, taking the chair beside the bed. She wondered at Bernadine sitting on the bed itself and why one of the servants wasn't feeding their honored guest as was their duty.

Perry laughed, wincing only slightly. "Perhaps I'm enjoying my confinement more than you did." He gave Augusta a broad wink that Bernadine couldn't fail to see. Augusta watched the healer shake her head, even blush, before smiling and looking away.

So, thought Augusta, unless she was mistaken—

"I guess we both have this lovely lady to thank for our recoveries," Perry added.

She was *not* mistaken. What a wonderful story that would make! A man brought almost to death's door and the woman who brought him back. Then a cloud darkened Augusta's thoughts. She couldn't imagine Perry saying he was going to order Bernadine around, nor could she see the healer becoming any man's servant.

She locked eyes with Bernadine a moment.

"I do thank you, Bernadine. It seems you were in two places at once."

"As you usually are," Bernadine countered, with a touch of admiration.

"I feel a bit slower tonight," Augusta admitted, though feeling herself blush at the healer's compliment. "What about your patient? Will he be out of bed in time for my wedding?"

"I think he could manage to make it to the chapel," Bernadine said, and Augusta did not miss the warm look that the woman cast over Rolf's friend.

"Good. I must speak with him now about . . . about the preparations. Unless you think he's too tired."

"No, not at all. I think he—"

"I'm going to clobber the both of you if you don't stop speaking as if I'm not in my right mind," Perry said, sitting up straighter on the bed and punching a pillow before placing it behind his back. "I can talk about the wedding. Although stuck here, I can be of little use."

Augusta fidgeted in her chair. She couldn't talk about Rolf in front of Bernadine. It was too embarrassing to be questioning Perry about her future husband. She shot the woman a quick glance.

"Millie is just outside the door. I'm sure she would enjoy the chance to chat with you."

Bernadine barely hesitated. "I, too, would like a word with my sister."

Standing, she placed the large bowl on the bedside table.

"Why don't you see if you can get some more of that into him while you talk," she suggested. "It will do him good."

"There you go again," Perry complained, but he gave her a parting grin.

There was a moment of awkward silence after the door closed.

"Well," Augusta said.

"Well," Perry agreed. "Some bastard laid us both low, did he not?"

"It would seem so. Though in truth you don't seem to be minding it too much."

Perry shrugged. "Bernadine is a fine healer."

"Not a bad looking woman either," Augusta added.

Perry looked her in the eye, then laughed. "No, not bad at all."

They relaxed then, back to the easy relationship they'd developed before the unknown archer's foul deed.

Augusta looked at the bowl. "You don't want me to feed you, do you?"

"No," Perry said, reaching for it, "but I'd better eat more or she'll . . ." He trailed off, looking a bit sheepish. Then he started to spoon in the stew, clearly demonstrating that Bernadine need not be sitting on his bed feeding him at all.

"About the wedding then?" Perry asked between mouthfuls.

Augusta sighed. What to say, what to say?

"I didn't really come here to talk about preparations," she admitted, then rushed on before she lost her nerve. "I want you to tell me about your captain. How is he . . . with women?"

Perry's spoon clattered into his stew.

"I mean, does he respect them? Or is he dismissive? Is he heavy-handed, despotic, tyrannical?"

Perry's eyebrows shot up higher with each word. He put the bowl back on the bedside table as Augusta took Bernadine's place on the bed. For the moment, he kept his mouth closed but she was determined to get answers.

"Is he threatening or domineering? Belligerent? Contentious?"

She was working herself up into quite a panic, when he took hold of her hand.

"Lady, what has got you in such a state?"

"I am marrying someone I hardly know."

"But that was the case yesterday as well. And that was the case when you entered into an arrangement with him. Are you thinking of backing out now?" Perry's face was full of concern.

"No," she assured him. "At least, I don't think so. But then the captain said something that caused me a measure of anxiety, and I . . ." *ran away like a scared lamb,* she thought

"What did he say?" Perry asked, sitting back but keeping hold of her hand.

"That as his wife, I had to obey him."

"Is that such a strange notion?"

"No, except how can I willingly agree to obey someone whom I have yet to befriend? What if what he expects of me is . . . cruel or . . . foolish?"

"Does he seem like either to you?"

She was silent a moment, thinking over each encounter they had had.

"No, but—"

"Would it help you to know that I have taken orders from him most of my adult life? For he was my superior when we fought for our king."

"And he was a good leader, I suppose."

Perry smiled. "He was. We had few men die because of his commands and many of us prospered. His orders always turned out to be in the best interest of those under him."

"That may be all right for naval officers, but I am to be his wife. So, I ask you again, in all earnestness, how does my future husband conduct himself with women?"

Perry coughed, cleared his throat, and coughed again.

"Rolf . . . well, that is . . ."

Oh dear, did he think she wanted him to tell her about their trysts with whores in various ports? That was irrelevant. As he looked into her face, she was sure he understood what she was really asking. Would Rolf be a kind and loving husband, respectful of the woman who'd been steward of her household? Unfortunately, his expression indicated that he wasn't entirely sure.

"He has a mother whom he has always held in high regard, as well as a sister to whom I've seen him show great fondness."

Augusta thought for a moment.

"What about women who are not family members?"

"Lady Augusta, he has not—" he paused a moment. "That is, in my memory, there have been no . . . , I mean, of course, there were, but so brief, . . . not the sort of." He shook his head. "Well, there you have it," he finished.

She was grinning at him now.

"There I have what? You have told me nothing even with all those words."

Perry grinned back. "I am simply not up to any more discussion. I fear, I must rest now." Scrunching down in the pillows, he tried to look tired.

She punched him in the shoulder.

"I'm starting to think he is such a blackguard, you are afraid to tell me."

Perry sat up again. "No, not that. It's only that, except for the easy women that . . . cannot believe I'm discussing this with you. Rolf would kill me."

He shook his head and started again, "Except for the kind of woman that one knows for only a very short while, he has never had any long-term alliance with a female. Never engaged or such. Yet his parents seem to have a happy marriage with mutual respect, from what I've seen. The rest, I suppose you'll have to teach him."

"Me?"

"You'll be his wife, the first and only. Surely, if you can run an estate like Thornbury, you can handle one captain who knows nothing but fighting and sailing and rough living."

Augusta took a deep breath. If she looked at it that way, yes, she supposed she could. She and Rolf would learn all about how to be a married couple together. Suddenly, she felt much better.

"Thank you. I am so glad I spoke with you, and equally glad that you are feeling better." She leaned forward conspiratorially, taking his hands again. "Perhaps you'll be learning about marriage yourself sometime soon?"

She heard the door open just as Perry laughed heartily and lifted up her hand to kiss it.

"*AH HM,*" ROLF CLEARED his throat. The sight of his best friend and betrothed couched together, touching, gave him a clearly uncomfortable feeling. This was Perry, though. Not Wesley, so he swallowed the flash of rage that had welled up into his throat.

"The two invalids are looking better," he observed, wishing his voice sounded more cordial.

Augusta got off the bed immediately, with a guilty look on her face that made the fury flare in him again. He quelled it once more. Right now, all he had to do was concentrate on keeping his fiancée alive for their wedding.

"I know you're feeling better, but it's getting late and you've been through quite an ordeal. I think you should retire to bed." He knew he was using the same tone with which he commanded his company of men, but he couldn't seem to help himself.

Gus looked hard at him. Then he watched her turn back questioningly to Perry who seemed to be nodding encouragingly. Whatever was between them was clearly to do with him, and he'd have to get it out of Perry later.

For now, he would see Gus safely back to her room. He'd already deposited a tray of food for her there himself, and it was being guarded by a serving girl until they returned.

She approached him, all traces of her earlier anger had disappeared.

"I will visit with you later," he promised Perry, and then, with his hand on the small of her back, he propelled Gus out of the room. The sisters who'd been chatting when he entered had disappeared.

In silence, they walked along the corridor to Gus's room. He wanted to say something to ease the strain that had sprung up between them since dinner, but he didn't know what. She seemed to be lost in her own thoughts.

When they reached her door, it was ajar, and he could hear Millie inside humming to herself. It stopped abruptly as he pushed the door farther open for Gus to enter.

She stepped over the threshold, breaking the contact of his hand on her back. Before he could even consider entering with her, she turned to face him, nearly bumping into his chest.

Looking down at her, it seemed to him that she was searching his face for something. He swallowed, hoping he would not be found wanting. Realizing he very much wanted her to like him, he smiled. Her glance went to his mouth where in a ruthless fight, one of his teeth had been knocked out. It had never bothered him before, but now he wished the gap were not there. What if it put her off entirely?

Yet to his amazement, she smiled back, and it reached her rich, sable eyes.

"You are correct, Captain, I am tired after all that's happened. And we have a big event ahead of us. I bid you goodnight."

Before he could think to respond, she closed the door firmly in his face.

Hm! At least she'd admitted he was right about something.

CHAPTER EIGHT

Perry looked neither hale nor hearty, but at least he was standing when Rolf answered the knock at his door. Rolf realized his best friend should still be abed, yet there he was upright, albeit leaning on the door jamb a trifle heavily.

"Come in before you fall in," Rolf said. "I am nearly ready."

"*Hah,*" Perry said. "You look paler than I do. Don't tell me you're nervous about taking a wife."

Rolf made a face. "Gus will make an excellent wife." Merely because he suddenly felt a bit indisposed didn't mean he did not want to be her husband.

"I agree. An outstanding one, I would think."

"Would you?" Rolf stood back as one of the male servants, William, came in with a freshly laundered shirt. Perry couldn't assist him in dressing, but after he had pulled on his narrow breeches, Rolf let the servant pin on his collar and help him slip into a cutaway tail coat in deepest blue.

With his hair tied back with a neat silk bow and his cravat tied in a mail coach knot, he sent William away.

As soon as the door shut behind the man, Rolf tugged on his top boots and asked as casually as he could, "What were you and my betrothed discussing so cozily in your chamber last night?"

Perry laughed instantly. "I will never tell the lady's secrets."

Rolf's froze, then purposefully relaxed his expression. "Truly? What secrets?"

Perry grinned. "You will have to discover the secrets of Lady Augusta yourself."

"I've been told that before," Rolf muttered, looking around the room to find the token he had brought on his long journey from Kent for his bride.

"Really, by whom?" Perry asked.

"Your Bernadine," Rolf responded, still rifling through his pack.

"Oh."

Seeing Perry's discomfiture apparent on his face, Rolf laughed. "You and your lady think alike."

"Stop saying she is *my* lady," Perry said, "though I'm sure her advice was good. What are you rummaging for like a boar hunting truffles?"

"The ring. I know I put it in here before we set out. Mother gave it to me. It's not grand, but I think Gus will like it."

He swore loudly when he got to the bottom of the bag. "I can hardly show up at the altar empty-handed."

"Perhaps you already took it out," Perry offered, beginning to search the room.

"Bloody hell." Rolf was fuming as he stuffed things back into his pack.

"I mean, really!" Rolf continued. "Do you think I would not remember if I did that?"

He stopped short as Perry walked to the window, picked up the ring from the sill and held it out to him.

"Come on," Perry said, clapping him on the back. "Let's get you married."

SILENT, UNMOVING, SOMEONE STOOD near the chapel's great double doors, watching and waiting for the bride and groom to arrive. The chances had all slipped by to stop the wedding—too many watching eyes, including men hired by the smart captain. A clenched fist, a sneer, an angry brow. The assassinations had been bungled outrageously. But there was still time.

A tentative smile. Yes, plenty of opportunity to break up the happy couple, or if need be, make sure an heir was never born, one way or another. Yet it had to be done while Thornbury was still full of guests, to provide cover and diversions. The would-be assassin slid inside unnoticed and took a seat to watch the ceremony.

AUGUSTA FELT SURPRISINGLY CALM. True, she'd already slipped getting out of the bath that morning, giving herself a throbbing right knee and a blossoming bruise. And she had caught her finger in the casement of her own window as she closed it. More throbbing, another bruise. Still, she was eager to get the wedding ritual over with. It was the wedding night that filled her with anticipation and dread.

"You look lovely, milady. Truly," Millicent said, as she smoothed Augusta's gown of blue silk, shot through with silver thread.

It had belonged to Lady Brenville, her mother, and had been carefully altered to look new and elegant, despite Augusta knowing it should have been sold years ago to pay for a month's worth of meat.

Her hair was up, with a crown of fresh flowers and lustrous pearls, put together by some of the ladies in

Thornbury. It made Augusta feel like a queen. In her hand, she held a handkerchief from her father, and around her neck was her mother's favorite necklace of gold chain with one precious sapphire hanging from it.

"Is it time, Millie?" Augusta asked, turning to look at her maid who was also dressed in her best.

Millie looked out into the hallway. A signal was given from one of the upstairs chamber maids.

"Yes, milady, it is. They'll all be waiting for you."

Especially Rolf.

She took a deep, calming breath, fingering the sapphire on its chain. She had been without a guiding female hand for so long, but today of all days, she wished for her mother to be there. Would her mother tell her what to expect not only that night but for the years of marriage that followed? She thought so. It would be a mother's duty to prepare her daughter for being a wife.

As if summoned, there was a quick rap on the door, and Helen sailed in without waiting for a reply.

"I'm sorry to barge in," Helen began, then she stopped and held her rounded middle, "but then the way I look," she continued with a laugh, "I barge everywhere I go."

"No," Augusta assured her. "You look especially lovely in your condition."

"Hopefully, you'll soon follow my example."

Augusta blushed. That was the plan, but to hear someone voice it, knowing what she and Rolf would do to create a baby, was nearly more than she could stand.

"I . . . I imagine soon, that is . . . I . . ."

"My mistress will have no trouble in that department, I'm certain," Millicent finished for her.

Helen turned as if she'd only just noticed a servant was in the room.

"Excuse me," Helen said, raising her eyebrows. She turned back to Augusta and smiled broadly. "I have no doubt you will be as fruitful as your cousin, my husband."

She patted her belly. "I only came to see if there was anything I could do to assist you."

Augusta had never known Helen that well, having visited her cousins less in recent years due to the lack of funds. And when she did, though they all lived together in a lovely manor, Helen was often away or busy with her children or so far along in a pregnancy that she was confined. Thus, Augusta knew her only as a beautiful lady who had captured James's heart. Now, she was discovering her to be kind as well.

"I thank you, Helen, truly I do. However, I think I am as ready as I'll ever be."

"And you do look ready, dear. You look lovely." Helen turned to leave. "I'll see you in the chapel, then." She paused and looked back, her gaze glancing at Millie before settling on Augusta. "If you need anything after the wedding, any assistance at all, please don't hesitate to ask me." Once more, she patted her protruding stomach. "I'm quite experienced in the matters of marriage, as you know."

Augusta blushed again as Helen left. She heard Millie mutter something under her breath.

"What did you say?"

"Nothing, milady. I'm just not sure I care for that particular member of the Brenville family."

"That's enough. I won't hear you talk disparagingly about my cousin's wife. She is truly a gracious lady."

"Or a meddlesome—"

"Millie!"

"Sorry, milady." She dropped her gaze to the carpet at Augusta's feet.

Augusta saw that Millicent was trying to look contrite but failing. Perhaps she had let the girl have too much leeway in her duties as her personal maid. When she was a wife, perhaps she would handle that differently.

"Let's go before I'm late for my own wedding."

"Oh, milady, they won't start without you. You're the jewel in the crown today, the pheasant at the feast, the rose in the garden, the—"

"I grasp your meaning, Millie. Let's go." Perhaps she would keep her just the way she was, after all. Another few moments and Millie was leaving her to the care of her father who awaited them at the bottom of the stairs.

"That was well done," Jerome Brenville commented, kissing his only daughter on the cheek. Augusta realized he was referring to the simple act of her making it down the stairs without once tripping. At least, it was a simple act for other folks. She watched Millie race ahead to get a seat in the chapel. Yes, without Millie, how many extra falls would she have taken down those very stairs?

"Father, I'm ready."

"I want to tell you, Augusta, that you look as lovely as your mother did the day she married me. I was honored to take her hand then and to take yours now. Rolf is a lucky man."

Augusta kissed her father on the cheek. Then he spoiled it all by adding, "But we're even luckier because he's got nearly as deep pockets as a prince."

"Father!" she admonished.

In a matter of a few yards, they were at the doors of the chapel, and she could think of nothing else except her "prince." Rolf had hired a harper for the occasion, and the lilting sounds coming through the open doors were lovely. That was one argument over wedding arrangements that he'd actually won, and Augusta was glad he had.

As for the rest of the ceremony, she had kept it simple. Rolf's requests to pay for something much more elaborate were shunned. Far too practical, Augusta could not waste his—and soon to be *her*—money, not when there were debts and servants to pay.

In any case, despite what Millie and her father said, she felt like an old bride who was better wedded with as little fanfare as possible.

Perhaps for the Christmas season, she and Rolf could go to London and present themselves at court during all the Michaelmas festivities. For now, she was content to wear her best dress and have her beloved father at her side.

When her eyes adjusted to the dimmer light of the chapel, she realized that it was quite full, not only with guests, but with some from the town who could get away from duties and squeeze in. She smiled at all the familiar faces as she walked up the aisle. Everything seemed just right, and she felt in her heart that she'd been meant to wait for precisely this day.

Searching farther up the aisle, she spied Rolf standing tall in an elegant indigo coattail, smiling encouragingly at her. And in an instant, she was struck by the notion that she was happy she'd waited for precisely this man.

He doesn't look like a grubby seaman today. Not at all.

Knowing it was improper, still Augusta thought for a moment of the other men who had been her suitors, of those she'd actually accepted. It was blasphemous, but she was glad they had not made it to the altar though she was sorry they'd died. Something about Rolf spoke to her heart. Something about him made her feel . . . comfortable, for lack of a better word. Because of that, she gave him a big smile as her father pressed her hand into her betrothed's.

Rolf's eyes widened, clearly bemused by the beaming grin on his bride's face.

He bent his head close to hers. "You look enchanting," he told her so only she could hear.

If possible, she felt her smile grow.

"And you are the picture of grace."

Now she blushed. Mercy! She hadn't even worried about tripping when she'd walked down the aisle.

Then the vicar began to speak. She found it hard to concentrate, thinking of how long it had taken for her to get to this day and thinking of what this meant to her and her father and to any children she would bear and even to the servants and the townsfolk. Then she heard her name and realized Rolf was speaking.

"Yes, I do," and he squeezed her hand.

He did, she thought. And more amazingly, he was turning to Perry and retrieving some token of his regard, as he called it. Turning back to her, he held out a gold band inlaid with small blue and green stones, which he slipped upon her finger. She stared at it amazed that he was really pledging his troth and sealing it with a circle of gold.

Then the vicar was speaking to her.

"Do you, Augusta Elizabeth Jerome Brenville of Thornbury, take Rolf—" Augusta coughed to cover up her dog's loud bark from outside the chapel's open window "—Henry Marsham, of Kent to be your husband?"

"Yes," she answered, looking into Rolf's deep brown eyes. "I do."

The vicar's words droned on and on until it was over, and she heard him say they were husband and wife. *How strange to hear them presented as one.* In less than half an hour, they had been joined as a couple for all the rest of their lives.

Augusta couldn't get over the fact that she felt not a whit different. She was a married woman. Nothing had changed, yet everything had changed.

Then, like a strong tide, the crowd of well-wishers surged forward to congratulate them. Rolf got pushed away in the process, and Augusta reached after him, sure there was supposed to be a kiss to end the ceremony. Over the heads of family and friends, she saw his look of concern though she felt no hint of danger in the familiar chapel.

In any case, it wasn't long before she sat down to sup with her new husband, enduring the age-old tradition of ribald jokes and lewd quips, even from James, Perry, and Wesley. She spent most of the meal blushing and eating food that could have been sawdust for all that she could taste it.

When the salaciousness had reached its peak, the trusted dames of Thornbury, many of whom had known Augusta since she was a child, stood up, along with Helen. Ignoring the catcalls with quiet dignity, the women approached her chair and bid her go with them.

Though some household servants joined them as they approached the doorway, including Millie, Augusta noticed that Bernadine was not among them, belonging neither to the town nor to the castle household nor to the family. In truth, Augusta would have been glad of her company and counsel.

As a group, they escorted Augusta out of the hall. She hesitated only a moment to look back at Rolf. He didn't have the wolfish grin that most of the men wore. Rather, he stared soberly straight at her, his eyes meeting and holding hers in a wordless communication of all that was to follow. She swallowed and turned away. Let him come, she thought, for I am ready.

Once she was in her chamber, however, it seemed that she was not allowed to be ready. At least, not until the women had fussed over her and undressed her then redressed her and took her hair down and brushed it out before styling it again. Millie put the finishing touches on her by applying perfume to her neck, inner elbows, and even the backs of her knees which quite shocked Augusta and caused the ladies to break out in laughter.

Lastly, Millie covered up her new nightgown with a gold brocade dressing gown that brought out the chestnut highlights in her hair.

When they were finally satisfied with her, they began on the room, making sure the fire was well stoked, lighting extra candles, and even adjusting the rugs so they were in front of the fire. Then they plumped the pillows and straightened the already smooth and clean-smelling sheets spraying them with the scent of violets.

Augusta was becoming more nervous by the minute with all their ministrations. Surely this one night could not be so important, could it? The butterflies in her stomach became nightingales.

At last, there was the sound of many feet and loud voices coming up the stairs and along the hall. To Augusta, it sounded like an army. The women all hushed expectantly, and Augusta jumped at the loud rapping at her door.

"It's time, milady," Millie said, in her characteristic shriek, causing her to clamp a hand over her own full lips. Then, against all decorum, Millie hugged her mistress before she and the rest moved *en masse* toward the door.

"Wait," Helen spoke up, "as the only female family present, I would speak with you alone." It was true. The aged aunties had remained downstairs, perhaps feeling distaste for these preparations.

Augusta nearly refused Helen. She could hardly bear the suspense any longer, especially when she heard the knocking again, this time more insistent. All she wanted was to be alone with Rolf, and to see that he hadn't changed any since the morning, certainly not into the lascivious Pan that these women seemed to be expecting.

"Now?" she questioned meekly.

"Yes, now," Helen insisted, taking hold of Augusta's hand and dragging her to the windowed sitting area where they could whisper privately behind the heavy drapes.

"I know that time is of the essence," Helen began.

Augusta knew at once that she spoke of the will and not the man pounding at her door.

"An heir must follow this union and with all due speed," she continued. "I know you have no mother to advise you, and though I am barely older than you," she added, "I have worlds of experience."

"I appreciate that, Helen, but I'm sure Rolf and I will manage just fine."

"Hah," Helen said with a shrug of her shoulders. "Men know nothing about begetting babies, only pleasing themselves and babies happen to come along." She had no malice in her voice as she added, "Yet if you handle yourself and your man correctly, Augusta, you'll have pleasure, too." She watched while Augusta blushed deeply. "And you shall have your babe. Here, take this," she said, pulling from her sleeve a small pouch, which upon examination proved to contain what looked to be ground seeds, some brown, some slightly pinkish. "These will ripen your womb and quicken your man's seed."

Augusta shook her head, nervous at the thought of "her man's seed." However, Helen pushed the small pouch into her hand.

"Just a little in your wine or ale and soon you will be bursting like I am. I've used it with success three times. And your womb is not as young as you could wish for a first babe. This will help. Trust me." She looked Augusta straight in the eye.

Augusta looked from Helen to the sachet in her hand. Helen was right. She should use whatever method was available to her. Time was of the essence and with a little help, perhaps she would conceive a child this very night.

"I wouldn't tell Rolf if I were you," Helen said, capturing Augusta's attention once again, "for I don't know about *your* man, but James would not like to learn that I thought he might need a little assistance. And with Rolf being a soldier," Helen shrugged again. "They have a reputation, but it's entirely up to you."

Suddenly, the curtains were tossed aside and Millie appeared just as Augusta closed her palm around the small sack.

"Milady?" she queried, wondering at the delay and looking from her mistress to Helen. "They will break the door down for certain."

"I'm ready." She took Helen's hand. "I thank you, and I will heed your advice."

"Good," Helen said, hugging Augusta close. In her ear before Helen released her, Augusta heard her say, "And enjoy yourself."

At that moment, one of the ladies opened the door, which was bowed by the pressure of the men outside. It seemed to Augusta that a sea of people flowed into her chamber. Indeed, it was difficult to locate her husband among them all as the men mixed with the women. Rolf must have been having the same trouble, for all at once she heard him.

"Silence," he roared, and Augusta thought it must be his finest officer-in-charge voice for instantly the crowd was quiet. Then he called out, "Gus."

"Here," she answered and the group parted to let her get close to her husband.

He took her hand in his and pulled her to his side. "Have you and your ladies finished?"

She nodded, still amazed at how he had the entire room full of people under control.

"In that case, let's get rid of them. I mean, that will be all, dear friends. We bid you good night."

There was much laughter as everyone shuffled out of the room to enjoy more drink and sweetmeats and merriment in their honor.

With everyone gone, Augusta stood stock still. Rolf dropped her hand as if touching her was suddenly too intimate now that there was just the two of them. She actually found it difficult to breathe, so great was her anticipation and fear. She was alone with Rolf . . . and he was her *husband!* This was it, their wedding night.

Rubbing her hands together nervously, she was surprised to find that she still clasped Helen's gift in one of them. Frantically, she looked around and espied by the bed the tray that she'd seen Millie carrying earlier.

On it were two large glasses of elderberry wine. She breathed a sigh of relief.

"What is it, my lady?" Rolf asked her, still not touching her but standing so close, he could hear the sigh that escaped her.

"I'm merely glad to see that there is wine," she admitted, "for I am quite thirsty."

"Then you shall slake your thirst. I made sure they were poured from a new bottle and guarded," he said, turning toward the tray.

"No," she exclaimed, pushing past him, nearly knocking him onto the bed. "I'll get it myself." She could hardly sprinkle the herb in if he were holding out her glass to her. "I am sure a husband is not supposed to wait on a wife on their wedding night."

"Really?" he asked. "I thought that's what I've been doing all night. Waiting."

She laughed, though it sounded high and false to her ears. She hurriedly sprinkled some of the seeds into her glass while her back was to him, and then a few more. At last, it was done, and she put the pouch down in the shadows at the back of the table. When she turned, she found Rolf so close behind her that she nearly upset the wine down his clean wedding shirt.

"You startled me." She lifted the glass to her lips.

"Wait." He stayed her hand with his own.

She gasped. Had he seen her put in the fertility aid?

"Let me sniff it first and make certain nothing is amiss," he said.

She glanced down and could see a small piece of husk on the top.

"Close your eyes," she urged him. "Your nose works better if you do so."

He frowned but did as she suggested and then held the wine close taking a long breath. "It smells fine," he said, "but let me—"

Augusta took a large sip before he could notice the seeds. His eyes popped open. Thinking of the act that was to follow, she gulped down another substantial draught of it, choked and spluttered, sending a spray of wine across his shirt.

Attempting to wipe it with nothing more than her finger tips, she nearly spilled the rest onto his boots.

"Gus," Rolf said, holding her arms still and away from him. Then he took the wine out of her hand and set it on the table. "You look even lovelier than you did at the ceremony today. But I would like to see more of you," he added. Releasing her, he began to unfasten his collar.

She blushed fervently. "Thank you," she murmured. "Do *you* want any wine?"

"No, my lady, I've had enough. Enough meat and drink, I mean. There is only one dish I care to sample tonight."

Her eyes grew wider. Should she start undressing, too, or would he do that for her? Would this whole ordeal last the entire evening or did the actual act happen quickly?

He brushed aside her hair, weaving his fingers into it as he did.

"I wish Millie had given you ale instead of wine. I don't want you going to sleep before we even start begetting our heir."

It was a good thing he'd taken the wine for she knew that his echoing of her thoughts would have made her choke again.

"You say it so matter-of-factly," she began, then she noticed the look in his eye. "You're teasing me."

"Yes," he said, leaning close and putting one of his strong hands behind her head, holding it still. "Right now, I'm not thinking of the heir to Thornbury castle at all."

"No?" she asked, her voice coming out as a husky whisper. The wine seemed to have spread through her quickly, making her whole body feel deliciously warm, and her head, light and worry free.

"There's only one thing I've been thinking about all evening. Actually, for about a week, maybe two." He bent down and kissed her.

Augusta felt herself melting against him, responding to his kiss with all the pent-up frustration of her years as a woman without a man. Her fears, along with her inhibitions, slipped away as easily as the wine had slipped down her throat. Now, she felt only the anticipation and excitement of a night with her husband.

Rolf undid the belt of her gown before pushing it off her shoulders to let it fall to their feet. He followed its path with his gaze, which took in her loose flowing nightdress of the sheerest gossamer.

He smiled. "Of everything I've seen you wear, my wife, I like this most of all."

Augusta shrugged self-consciously, feeling her cheeks aflame. Having sent to Bristol for it, Rolf had gifted it to her a week earlier in private. The deep indigo echoed her wedding gown, but the transparent fabric clearly indicated it was made for the bedroom. She had folded it away for this night.

As she moved, it brushed against her hip or her breast, revealing a hint of what was beneath.

He took a fold of the fabric between his thumb and finger. "You should wear it all the time."

That broke her nervousness, and she laughed. "I would do well running my estate in this."

His face went expressionless for a moment. "It's *our* estate now, Gus."

She looked at his hand, still holding the side of her gown. "Yes," she breathed.

"How does that make you feel?" he asked.

Augusta looked into his face. Her answer clearly mattered to him. If it were crucial to her that he give her an heir, it was critical to him that she make his claim on Thornbury legitimate. He did not want to be treated as an outsider, as a conquering soldier who only held the land by her grace. She could see and understand that.

"It makes me feel as though I have a partner," she told him, with hope that it would be true. "Someone to share the burden of the problems that arise, as well as the joys." Then she remembered his words that had caused her to seek Perry's counsel. "Although in the eyes of the law, we are not nor ever will be equal partners."

He remained silent.

She wanted him to tell her that they would share in all the decisions, but how could he utter such a radical statement? He was a man, an officer, and she a mere woman.

In answer, Rolf bunched up the fabric still in his hand, getting a good grip on his wife and pulling her against him.

A wedding demanded a bedding, she thought, remembering an old saying.

"Truly, Gus, I will hold up my end of the bargain. Let me give you an heir. We will both enjoy it, I promise you." He brought his lips against hers once more.

Augusta spirits deflated like a popped soap bubble. He had let the opportunity to reassure her go past because he agreed with the letter of the law. He really did intend to give her a baby, his own flesh and blood, and in return he was going to dismiss her as steward of Thornbury, as if she'd never had a capable thought in her head or was fit to do aught else except breed.

Even the heady wine could not maintain her warmth in the face of her qualms. She wrapped her arms around herself, forming a wedge between them.

He lifted his mouth from her unyielding one.

"Gus?"

"Very well, my lord," she said, all pretense of affection gone. "Let's get to procreating. After all, isn't that what this is all about? All the people of Thornbury, castle and town, are happy for us tonight. And to keep them happy, I would do anything , even marry *you!* They're all downstairs hoping that we're up here making the heir that will keep everything exactly as it is. My father will keep his castle. The servants will keep their jobs and get paid regularly. The town will prosper. If only we make a baby."

In a fit of vexation, Augusta wrenched herself from his embrace and jumped on to her bed. She spread herself out, like a five-pointed star.

"Okay, Rolf, I'm ready."

She didn't dare look at his face. The silence stretched interminably between them. Even without him speaking, she could feel his annoyance over her words and her attitude. She was not the passionate wife he had hoped for, just a compliant breeder. She closed her eyes, awaiting him.

The next thing she heard was the door to their chamber opening and crashing closed.

CHAPTER NINE

Augusta didn't go downstairs early in the morning as she usually did. Rather, she hid miserably in bed, even keeping Millie at bay with the excuse that a new bride had the right to some time alone. A new bride, Augusta reflected, which was exactly what she did not feel like. She felt like a fraud.

She'd spent a nearly sleepless night, huddled in a ball in her big bed that had never seemed more of a mockery for the lady of the manor. She'd spent the night naked for the first time in her life, after she'd ripped off the beautiful, sensual nightgown and tossed it in a heap on the floor. *With loathing!*

Did everyone know they hadn't spent the night together? She feared that humiliation most of all. Of course, she would be blamed as unlovable! Had Rolf gone straight back downstairs after he'd slammed the door on her sarcastic offering of her splayed body for impregnation?

Finally, by midday, Augusta could stand it no longer. She dressed herself with care and styled her hair simply but neatly so as not to require Millie. She thought about going to see Perry but was too humiliated in case he knew. Instead, she went stealthily downstairs, hoping to encounter no one before she reached the makeshift lean-to that was being used as a stable until they could rebuild what had burnt.

Luck seemed to be on her side as she found only a dozing stable boy who, when awakened by his harried mistress, swiftly hitched her horse to her favorite carriage.

With her dog on the small back seat and the reins in hand, Augusta froze. It was not that long ago that she'd been on her deathbed. Moreover, the assassin was still out there. It would be folly to ride out alone. If only Perry were well enough to ride, or if Rolf . . .

Frustrated by her predicament but desperate to escape for a little while, Augusta urged her horse out of the main gate and along the road to the town. She was progressing slowly and carefully, when Wesley rode up from the other direction.

"Greetings, Coz," he said, turning his horse and keeping pace beside her.

"Hello, Wesley," she returned. His overly cheerful countenance was about the last thing she could stand. "Come along, gee-up," she urged, giving the reins a short snap.

"Hold up," he said, after they'd gone a furlong in silence. "I'll ride with you."

Without asking, he dismounted. She was forced to stop as he tied his horse to the back of her carriage.

"There, that's infinitely more companionable," he said, taking the reins from her hands.

She neither allowed nor disallowed his statement. However, given the current circumstances, she realized the benefit of having a strong man by her side should she need protection.

After a short while, he asked, "Where are we going?"

"I'm not sure. I simply wanted to get out of the castle."

"*Ah.*" He stayed silent for a few more minutes as they went through the main street of the town, and she waved to folks who greeted her. Then they started up the hill where Rolf and his men must have seen their first view of Thornbury.

What was Rolf doing now? she wondered. Had he told Perry that she was unreasonable? That he was rethinking his arrangement? How would they pay him back for the repairs he'd already paid for?

She stopped suddenly.

"Shall we go toward Stafford's grange? Speedily, the way we did when we were youngsters?"

He looked puzzled, perhaps wondering at her mood, but he readily agreed. Her lightweight, sturdy-wheeled curate cart could travel quite quickly, and in a moment, they were flying down the other side of the hill, her horse trotting at a decent pace. A part of her wanted to keep on going, over the next hill and the next. After all, she'd given the castle everything for her entire life. Hell's bells, she'd even married for it.

They galloped over the hills for a few minutes until the horse tired, and Wesley let it come to a stop. "What say you, Augusta? If I remember, there are gooseberries around here somewhere?"

"Yes," she agreed absentmindedly, letting him catch her as she jumped down from the seat. "I'm not sure if there will be any left on the bushes this late. In any case, I didn't bring anything to collect them in."

She wiped a fly away from her forehead with the back of her hand, and her new ring grazed her skin. *A token of his regard.* Just yesterday, Rolf had pledged his troth. Today, her chest felt heavy with sorrow.

"Why so melancholy, Coz?" Wesley asked, tilting her chin up so she would have to look at him. "You don't seem like a woman who has just married a very wealthy man in the king's favor."

"No," she asked, "what do I seem like? Perhaps like a woman whose new husband cares more for the power he has gained than for her sensibilities." She jerked her head away from Wesley's hand and looked back toward her beloved Thornbury. "Do I seem like a woman whose husband walked out on their wedding night?"

And with that, she began to cry in earnest, as she had needed to since she'd heard the door slam the night before.

"Oh, Augusta," Wesley said, taking her in his arms. He rocked her gently without asking any more questions.

In her line of vision, just past his right shoulder, she saw a rider on horseback who paused on the crest above them before turning and disappearing out of sight. If she didn't know better, she would swear it was her new husband. Yet that couldn't be. Rolf would have charged down the hill and confronted them. That was, if he cared a fig for her.

ROLF KNEW HE SHOULDN'T be surprised, but he was shaken nonetheless. He'd seen it with his own eyes—his wife in the arms of another man. Wesley! Just as he'd feared weeks ago when the man's name first came off Gus's lips.

Clearly, she was in love with her cousin. No, it hadn't surprised him. A woman didn't reach Gus's age with her heart unfettered. Nevertheless, he'd thought she would dismiss any such attachments given the reality of their marriage and given the need to satisfy her grandfather's conditions to keep Thornbury.

The first person he encountered after riding hell bent back to the castle was James, out for a stroll with Helen delicately holding onto his arm.

"Greetings," they both called out to him as he went past.

He only nodded, not trusting himself to speak and particularly not wanting to bear witness to such a happy marriage.

Dismounting, he tossed the reins to one of the stable hands, still pondering whether he should have ridden down the hillside and confronted the pair. It would have ended in a challenge, he feared. His slaughtering a Brenville in a duel was not the way to keep peace or win over the people of Thornbury. He had a brief word with Peter and then headed inside.

Rolf wanted Perry's counsel, and it didn't take long to find him seated on a divan in the cozy parlor off the main hall, deep in conversation with Bernadine. Stopping at the sight of them laughing and talking, he noted how closely their heads were bowed together. He had never experienced that with Gus, though he'd wanted to. Now, it was too late. Too late if she was being intimate with Wesley.

Feeling awkward standing in the doorway and hating to disturb Perry's happiness, Rolf forced his feet forward. Here at Thornbury, he was still an outsider and nearly everyone's interests were tied to Gus. Only Perry could give him advice for his own good.

"Good day," he said to them both.

So wrapped up in each other, they looked surprised to find there was anyone else in the room. Still, Perry and Bernadine each gave him a share of their happiness with a welcoming smile.

He wished he could offer one in return, but all he could think of was Gus in Wesley's arms. Gus who'd offered herself to him the night before like a human sacrifice, making a mockery of the passion he'd intended to share with her.

"I beg your pardon, Bernadine, but I must speak with your patient."

"Certainly, my lord," she acquiesced. Rising, she reached down to press Perry's arm, letting her hand linger there as she insisted he not stand on ceremony.

When Perry took hold of the healer's hand and openly kissed her fingertips, Rolf felt the gesture like a kick to his gut.

"I will find you later," his friend told Bernadine, bringing another smile to her lips as she bid them both good day.

"Are you going to sit?" Perry asked, but Rolf shook his head, too agitated to stay put.

"I'll just pace in front of you like a trapped tiger," he said.

Perry sobered at his friend's tone. "I'd offer to pace with you, but I'm not quite up to it yet."

"You seem much better though," Rolf said, taking a long look at him.

"I've had great care and a reason to recover quickly. But you didn't wish to talk to me simply to marvel at my recovery, did you?"

"No," Rolf admitted. Still he remained silent, unwilling to put into words and make real what he'd seen.

Perry crossed his arms, waiting. "Maybe a drink would loosen your tongue."

However, Rolf merely shrugged and kept pacing.

"You have a good wife in your Lady Gus," Perry observed.

"Wrong on both counts," Rolf said bitterly. "She is neither a good wife, nor is she mine apparently."

He stopped and looked out the window at the grounds, some still unkempt, some restored for the wedding. Then he turned and let his gaze circle the comfortable, albeit shabby room.

For the first time, the Tudor castle that had captivated him upon first viewing it seemed to be merely a building on a piece of land. Would he have been better off marrying some wide-eyed young lass who would worship him?

Perry was staring at him, slack-jawed, as if he had two heads.

"What?" Rolf asked. "Are you finally at a loss for words?"

"You've been wedded for less than twenty-four hours. It seems rather brief a time to decide whether Augusta makes a good wife."

"Even if I've already found her in the arms of another man."

Perry's expression was one of incredulity. "Between your wedding night and noon?"

"Precisely." Rolf felt a misery that was out of keeping with his usual dealings with female attachments. He had never cared a tuppence for any of them. For the first time, however, he realized how it would feel if he did really care. He didn't like it—not one bit.

"With whom?" Perry asked, still sounding doubtful of his friend's words.

"Wesley, of course, that simpering, flawless, golden-haired, clean . . ."

Perry actually started to smile, which made Rolf feel like hitting him.

"What the hell is so amusing?" he asked.

Perry shook his head slowly, still looking amused.

"The man is family, her cousin, for Christ's sake. He could have been wishing her well or comforting her for any number of reasons. Admit it, all you saw was an embrace and your mind has run wild."

Rolf thought hard for a moment, a small feathery feeling of hope barely brushing him. "He held her chin, and I believe there was some rocking motion going on."

"There, you see. More like he was comforting her over something," Perry went on. "If you'd seen their mouths brush or him nuzzling her neck, that would be another story," he continued. "Where were they?"

"Miles away, toward that granary we saw when we first arrived. I was out riding and saw them cross my path, so I followed. They were together on Gus's curate, riding like the devil," Rolf added.

"Did she see you, following her and spying on her?"

"I wasn't spying," Rolf explained, "and besides with an assassin still around, I had to make sure she was all right. I'm fairly certain that she saw me."

"Why didn't you go and escort her home? For that matter, why wasn't she out riding with you?"

Finally, Rolf sat down hard in the chair opposite, feeling exhausted suddenly from his sleepless night. "We argued last evening. I spent the night in my own chambers."

"I know you outranked me when we served, but I must say, you are a clod."

Rolf stretched out fully in the chair that seemed too small and put his arm over his eyes. He said nothing.

Perry persisted. "Do you believe her safe with Wesley? For I'll ride after her myself if need be."

"Nay, she looked exceptionally safe in his arms," he said, still keenly tasting the jealousy like a bitter fruit. "Besides, they went right through the town together. If he is behind the murder attempts, he'd be foolish to do anything after being seen alone with her."

"Still—" Perry persisted.

"Do not worry overmuch. I sent Peter out immediately to check on her."

Perry said nothing more.

Finally, Rolf uncovered his eyes and looked at him. "What now?"

Perry shook his head. "You're not acting like Lord of the Manor."

"Christ sakes! I've only been one less than a day."

"Just as Lady Augusta has only been a wife the same amount of time. You can help each other. She knows all there is to know about running this castle. You know all there is to know about . . ."

"Yes?" Rolf queried when Perry trailed off.

"About yourself," he finished with a grin. "You can help her be a good wife to you. If that's what you want."

Rolf thought of Gus, her genuinely good soul, her quick mind, not to mention her shapely body in her nightgown. "Of course that's what I want. I wedded her, didn't I?"

"Then I suggest you tell her that," Perry added.

He *had* told her the night before. She'd said she wanted a partner to share the burden, and he'd said . . . he'd said he'd give her a baby. Not exactly what she'd hoped to hear, he reasoned.

Jumping up, Rolf charged out of the room, hearing Perry's encouragements chasing after him.

"GUS, I WOULD SPEAK with you." Rolf found her in the king's solar, sitting doing nothing. Absolutely nothing. The very oddity of her not being busy at some task struck him at once. He rarely saw her resting. At his entrance, she visibly stiffened in her chair.

"I've got too much work to do," she said, though the table in front of her was glaringly empty.

He smiled at her words, glad to know she was a terrible liar.

"What?" she asked. "Why do you smile?"

Apparently, his expression annoyed her tremendously. Rolf had been thinking what to say to her since his conversation with Perry. "I'm smiling because I have found you, my wife."

"Wife," she repeated, glowering at him, the word sounding like a curse.

"Yes," he said, drawing her up out of the chair by both hands. He pulled her to him. Still, she was stiff and unyielding, and all his well-rehearsed speeches went right out of his head. "Truly, I am sorry for last night."

She looked down, sideways, anywhere but at his face until he had to take her face in his hand. Her eyes were large and overly bright with unshed tears.

"Gus, shall we try again tonight?"

She closed her eyes, hiding her thoughts from his view. Then she shook her head and he released her.

"Try what?" she practically whispered. "Try to make an heir?"

"No," he protested. "I mean, yes, we will but . . . not merely that." He gathered his thoughts. "I would like to give you a proper wedding night."

She shook her head again. "Everything was perfect last night. How can I ask my women to do all that again?"

He laughed. "They were just a nuisance and a distraction, my lady. All that we need, we carry on ourselves, I promise you. If you want aught else, I'm sure we can manage. I can light the fire, you can bring the wine." He took her in his arms again, and this time, she felt more pliable. "Simply leave your hair loose. That's how I like it best. And wear whatever you wish. You shall not stay clothed for long."

At that remark, she finally smiled, and a measure of triumph soared through him. She still intended to honor their contract at least, though he was sure she was harboring doubts about him as her husband.

"I want you to know that I will consult you in all matters to do with Thornbury." He looked nearly as surprised as she did when he blurted this out.

"Really?" she asked, placing a warm hand upon his chest.

It was going well, Rolf thought. "Truthfully," he said. "Though ultimately all the decisions will quite naturally fall to me to make, I will welcome your musings."

"My musings!" Gus's face went nearly purple as she flared with rage.

It was *not* going well, Rolf thought. He was a reasonable man. He kept giving in a little, but then she wanted more. Gus wanted to run her family's estate as if he did not exist. It would not be tolerated. He let his arms fall away from her.

"I did not mean to offend. I have commanded a ship of men as we went into battle, I think you can trust me to govern this castle and all who live here."

"It is not a matter of my trusting your judgment, either in battle or in governing. Don't you see? I have lived here my whole life. The people trust my family and work in earnest for us. They don't know you. You can't simply arrive and expect their allegiance and their trust. Country folk, as you know, can be highly suspicious. Things are running so smoothly at Thornbury, with no insurrections in living memory. You are a stranger to them, a sailor no less."

"Is it really the trust of the people that worries you?" he asked. "Or that you don't want to give over the reins of control to your husband?"

AUGUSTA WANTED TO RIP her hair out. No, she wanted to rip *his* hair out—his long, dark, clean hair.

"All right, sir, let us say for a moment that you ingratiate yourself with all who live and work at Thornbury, and even the townsfolk. Let us say that you have everything running smoothly. You are counting sheep, if you like, collecting the peasants' coin when they use the mill, taking your share of crops and livestock while ensuring a good market for the townspeople. What would you suggest I be doing while you are thus occupied?"

"You will be having our baby."

She rubbed her hand over her eye. "Yes, yes, I will be *enceinte*. Then what?"

"What?" he asked.

"I've seen expecting women who at the same time till the fields, do the laundry, pick crops. I have always worked. What will I do while I'm awaiting the baby's arrival?"

"Nothing," he said firmly. "The heir is too important to both of us. You will rest and relax and be healthy and bring forth a baby."

"Rest for forty weeks?"

He merely shrugged.

"All right," she said through clenched teeth. "Let us say that I relax my way to an heir. Then what? What will be my place after that?"

"Why, you'll be his mother."

"*His* mother! He might be a she, by God. And I will be a good mother to her. But what else?"

"My wife," he added. "You'll be my wife, naturally."

"And that means?"

He sighed with exasperation. But then he hesitated and narrowed his eyes.

"My father runs his Marsham estate, and my mother seems to be busy all day."

"Doing what?" Augusta asked him.

He frowned, clearly considering.

"Why, you must know," he said, his brow clearing. "You're a woman. Do whatever women do all day after they become wives."

She felt a throbbing in her temples and thought she might have an apoplectic fit.

He didn't seem to notice. "I'm sure we could write to my mother for assistance with this." He smiled at her, looking certain that he had solved the problem.

"Perry was correct. You simply don't know what a wife does, perhaps because your mother died. You merely need guidance."

Augusta stood frozen, uncertain how to respond without raising her tone. At last, she found her calm voice. "Perry and you discussed my wifely abilities?"

"Not like that, Gus." He swallowed, looking sickly. "I mean, I merely want you to be happy in your place, in your new situation."

"I understand." And she did. All too well. "I don't know what to say, my lord. I really don't."

"Just say, thank you."

She paused. Was he jesting with her? If not, he was incredibly dense.

"Thank you," she said. And when he started to reach for her again, she added, "Thank you for showing me what a boorish individual you are with such limited imagination. You really are nothing but a coarse sailor."

Augusta started for the door. She doubted she could throw him out so she would have to be the one to leave.

"I am something else," his voice was quiet yet it stopped her. "I am your husband."

She turned back to him. "Clearly, that was a mistake." For the briefest moment, she felt trapped like a warble in a snare. Then a thought occurred to her. "We have not consummated the marriage. The Church will consider a petition for annulment."

She watched his face pale and felt her own fear wash over her at what she was thinking.

"I shall speak with my father directly."

"Gus," his voice stopped her again, and he moved toward her. "What about your grandfather's will? What about making an heir? If you're not careful, you'll lose everything. And not only you. Can you do that to your father after he has gone to all this trouble to see us wed?"

Her shoulders wilted, and she put her face in her hands. Yet she was determined not to cry? He was correct. She was letting her pride get in the way of the future of Thornbury.

"I don't want to keep you by force or through necessity because of that damned will," he said. "However, I would very much like to keep you." He put his arms around her.

CHAPTER TEN

Augusta pulled away from his embrace and instantly saw frustration blanket his features. He was not a man who was used to being denied. And in truth, she had no reason to, except for the nagging feeling that there could be so much more to this union than she had at first supposed.

Though it was all she ever had wanted, she now wanted more than a husband who could save her home and give her children.

She wanted a companion, not an overlord. She wanted someone who would share the responsibilities that she had borne for so long, but not shoulder them on his own. At the same time, she wanted someone to make light of the work with his smile, his banter, his love.

She could see how all of this was possible with her new husband, but he seemed to see her as merely a child bearer and his bedfellow.

"Gus," he said. "I am truly terrible with speeches. In that you're correct. I'm a soldier, not a diplomatic man. From the moment I open my mouth to make matters better, I seem to only make them worse between us."

"I cannot acquiesce to being pushed aside from the very tasks I've done all my life."

He sighed. "You did them because there was no one else. Your father apparently doesn't have a head for business, you have no brothers, and your mother passed. Now, you have me. We can . . . work together to restore Thornbury, if that is what you wish."

She looked at him. Was he compromising? His warm grin appeared. Either he was offering a compromise or he was maneuvering into position to triumph over her.

"Perhaps when we know each other better, we will trust one another's abilities more," he added. "Whereas I want you to hand me the ledgers and keys to the castle and then not interfere, you want me to provide the funding and the heir and then carry on as if I am not here. Neither seems like a very wise solution for two reasonable people."

Wasn't that what she had been feeling, too? Perhaps they really wanted the same thing after all but were simply going about it in different ways. Were she to let Rolf in to her body and soul, then he would perhaps let her in to his heart and mind. She decided right then and there what to do. Perhaps it had been his come-hither grin, but she could wait no longer.

"I do not wish to be difficult, Rolf, nor do I want to have our marriage annulled. Tonight, we shall share our marriage bed."

HE HADN'T MEANT TO be late to sup with his wife that night, but he'd taken special care with his grooming, wanting to look as good to her as she did to him.

Finally, after combing his hair for the second time, he'd tossed the comb down in disgust. Thank God Perry couldn't see him primping and behaving like a woman.

However, it was him and not Perry who had married and who would enjoy his wife that night. She had said it so matter of factly that he had nearly missed it. "We'll share . . . pardon, my lady? What are you saying about tonight?"

He had made her repeat her statement.

"We shall consummate," she had said the word slowly, enunciating each syllable and looking as serious as he felt elated.

He had wanted to take her right then, to strip off all the layers that hid her, and, most of all, he had wanted to please her in the best way he knew how.

God, he ached to make love to this woman. From their brief physical moments, he knew that she was totally untried, totally innocent—it thrilled and terrified him. Her entire sexual experience would begin with him. Tonight.

He knew a sense of satisfaction when he entered the dining room, looking to where Gus always sat. Perhaps it was the dimness of the hall and the candlelight playing a trick, but she looked somehow different. He saw her start in her seat. Clearly, she had been waiting for him. And she gave a small smile meant only for him, before looking back down at her food.

He moved hurriedly to his seat next to her.

"I apologize for my tardiness," Rolf told her, taking her hand, looking at her sweet capable fingers, then kissing her palm lightly.

"Apology accepted," she said, just before dropping her spoon with a great clatter against her plate.

Everyone seemed to look at them at once, and Rolf released her hand. Even Perry was smiling widely at them from his position a few seats down.

"You look . . .," he paused as he truly looked her over and the word stuck in his throat like a chicken bone, but he said it anyway, "lovely."

Good God! What had she done to her face and hair? Both were an unnatural whiteness that he'd only seen at court among the ladies in waiting. Her sweet face, usually so healthy, appeared like the chalky cliffs of Dover in his home county. And her hair, normally plain brown—sometimes with glorious reddish highlights—was nearly white, while the texture was all wrong.

He couldn't help himself. He reached up and touched an errant lock. It was stiff! Giving her what he hoped looked like a genuine smile, he had a feeling his lips were stuck to his teeth. Quickly, he took his seat.

Looking down at the first course set before him, he began to eat. With Gus, one just never knew. Still, tonight would be their first night together. Moreover, despite her odd appearance, he would enjoy himself and make sure she did the same. Glancing at her again, he hoped to catch her eye, but she was studying the pastry on her slice of game pie and was avoiding looking back at him.

Now what? He winced. He shouldn't have touched her hair and not said anything. After all, clearly it was meant to be stylish. Some was piled up on her head in a thick generous mound, and some locks were left hanging down. But all of it was definitely pasty. Taking another sideways glance, he was happy not to detect any extra sections of horse hair woven in. He'd seen that often enough in London and thought it looked ridiculous.

After a few more minutes of silence between them, she excused herself and fairly flew from the hall, her dog at her heels. She crashed her shoulder into the edge of the door jamb as she left. He winced again before listening to her thumping up the main stairs.

Waiting, he held his breath, hoping that she didn't stumble and come plunging back down head over heels.

No one else seemed to have noticed anything odd. He pushed what was left of his food around on his plate and then excused himself. Perry still grinned like a fool, but Rolf now realized that he was a bit in his cups and was actually chatting up the woman across from him, who was nearly old enough to be his mother. No doubt he was simply missing Bernadine who had not been invited to the dining room. Yet.

Heading up the stairs two at a time, Rolf knocked first at her chamber. There was no answer. Boldly, he pushed open the door. No Gus. Where was she?

Next, he looked in the solar to no avail. Empty. He even returned to his own chamber, thinking for one foolish moment that she might be awaiting him on his bed. Alas, not so.

Lastly, he went to the bathing room, though he knew she'd already bathed before dinner as was her custom. Outside the door, his namesake slept contentedly, his snout upon his paws.

Then he heard her, first crying, a loud sobbing that echoed in the tiled room, and then splashing.

Bollocks! He imagined her so distraught over having to lie with him that she was trying to drown herself. Opening the door without knocking, Rolf feared he was correct. For there was Gus by the light of one candle, fully clothed, kneeling over the bath with her head submerged in the water.

Running to her side, he took her by her slender shoulders and wrenched her backward. She fell onto him, her soft bottom landing on his lap as he sat heavily upon the hard floor.

She didn't say anything or look at him. She just sat there, water dripping all over them both, and she was still crying. He forcibly turned her round so she was facing him.

What an unholy mess! Her face was now streaked with white paste and her hair was half white, half brown. The top of her gown was entirely ruined.

Belatedly, he realized that she hadn't been trying to drown herself, merely washing her hair.

"Gus, what the hell is going on?"

She took in a deep breath, but what came out was little more than a whisper. "I wanted to look special for you tonight."

Her words hit him like a fist in the gut. "You always look special," he lied.

She shook her head, dismissing his words.

"Millie told me about the style at court. The ladies use a flour mixture to hold it up."

"I've seen them," he said quietly.

"Yes, naturally, you would have." She tried to keep the bitterness from her tone. "When we tried to use the bellows to blow flour into my hair, it didn't work at all. It turned out like biscuit dough, but I figured it was supposed to be this way. Millie has never actually seen it. She merely heard about it from her man, Jared, whose sister worked in London last season. Then I saw the look on your face. And the way you touched it."

She shuddered. "I realized it was a mistake. And I *had* wanted to be perfect for you."

For *him*? What had he done to deserve perfection, let alone deserve Gus just as she was? Kind and intelligent. What matter that she was a bit clumsy? He hugged her to him until they were both covered in flour paste. And right then, he was enjoying the feeling of her squirming in his arms and of her round bottom on his thighs. He grew hard, but she didn't seem to notice.

"You should finish your meal and let me clean myself up," she said, pushing off his lap and standing up so quickly, she nearly tumbled back into the tub.

Rolf grabbed at her flailing arms just in time.

"I have lost my appetite for anything but you." He lifted her messy face to his and kissed her with all the desire he felt. He couldn't help slipping his tongue between her lips as he had not done earlier.

She seemed immobilized for a moment before pressing against him. Then slowly, she touched his tongue with her own.

Grabbing the cheeks of her bottom, one in each hand, he held her up against his own hard sex. "Let us get clean together. This time, it is I who is demanding to bathe."

He built up a fire in the fireplace. Then he filled the great tub with hot water while his wife watched it all silently and with appreciative eyes. At last, when the room was warm and steamy, he undressed her, layer after layer—gown, petticoats, corset, chemise, stockings—until she was standing before him, naked at last.

Her skin was all hills and valleys in the flickering light. She *was* beautiful. Incredibly so. Even streaked with flour paste. How had he missed it for these past weeks?

He didn't trust himself to touch her, yet he did just that, although only to take hold of her fingertips and lead her to the bath. She never took her eyes off of his. And when he smiled, he saw an answering smile in her sparkling caramel-brown eyes.

Rolf undressed hurriedly though he didn't join her in the tub immediately. Instead, he found the chamomile soap that his lady so favored and he began to wash her, lovingly, reverently. And miracle of miracles, she let him.

AUGUSTA COULDN'T REMEMBER THE last time she was rendered speechless and breathless, but she was both. Her new husband was naked, on his knees, leaning over the tub and rubbing a cloth up and down her back. She felt as if she had no bones, all of her melting into the hot soapy water.

He brought the cloth around the front of her and gently wiped her face until it was utterly clean. She watched the bob in his neck go up and down as he swallowed before rubbing the cloth over the front of her shoulders and then down between her breasts.

For a moment, she could look at him unabashedly while his gaze was fixed solely on her naked breasts. His expression of pleasure sent waves of joy through her.

Suddenly, his gaze caught her own, his eyes looking at hers questioningly.

She wasn't sure of the question exactly, but she nodded almost imperceptibly. Whatever Rolf wanted to do was perfectly fine with her.

Slowly, he rubbed the washcloth over her breasts and she gasped. As he circled her nipples, the roughness of the cloth rasped over her sensitive peaks, driving her to distraction.

When he pushed the washcloth lower with an agonizing lack of haste, deliberately teasing her, Augusta had to grip the sides of the tub and bite her lip to stop from moaning. Loudly. Raising her hips toward his movements in an effort to hasten the next delight, she held her breath, bit her lower lip, and closed her eyes.

When he finally brushed over her soft brown curls with the cloth, she felt she would faint in the water. Instead, she lay her head back and ever so slightly spread her legs apart. He could not see into the soapy water, not in the dim candlelit chamber, so he kept his eyes on her face and was washing her by touch. And, oh, what a touch he had!

Augusta let herself sigh out loud as he parted the lips to her woman's center and again, stroked the washcloth over her tingling flesh.

"Rolf," she breathed, rising up again, hoping to increase and intensify the sensations that were building inside her.

"Gus," he answered, his voice husky. Yet he said nothing else, as he let the cloth slip from his hand and instead ran his palm over the mound of her desire.

"Rolf," she exclaimed again.

When he touched her in so intimate a fashion, she feared she would fall unconscious and drown in the tub. As his sensual ministrations continued, she felt an intense pressure building in her trembling body.

"I want . . . I want you to . . . just keep doing that," she murmured.

"I wasn't planning on stopping," he assured her. And he didn't. He lifted one hand to her breast, to rub the back of his knuckles against her sensitive skin, while his other hand continued its sweet assault on the throbbing center of her being.

Lifting her hips nearly out of the water, she rode his hand until the pent-up pressure exploded through her, up and along her spine, making her pant with exertion and call out something unintelligible.

Then Rolf's strong arms were around her. After kissing her quite thoroughly on her parted lips, he climbed into the tub behind her and began to rinse her off. When he was done with her, she was lying back on his naked chest, clean and warm, and exhilarated.

"I think we should get out of this ridiculous floury mess and retire," she said.

"But I just got in, wife, and I know how much it pleases you more than anything for me to bathe."

She elbowed him in the ribs.

"Oomph," he said. "Indeed, I am clean enough," he proclaimed, "Let me rinse the paste from my arms and face, and then, the marriage bed awaits us."

Before he could stop her, she scrambled from the tub, surprised at keeping her feet under her and not sprawling across the wet floor as she had done many a time. Grabbing for a drying cloth, she wrapped it around herself and faced her grinning husband.

"If the tub was that wondrous," she told him, "I can barely imagine what the bed will be like. I say you are clean, Rolf. Now hurry."

And he did.

CHAPTER ELEVEN

Augusta had no way of knowing that the next day was very nearly her last. It started out with sunlight streaming through the curtain they'd forgotten to draw closed the night before, and it progressed with kissing her husband and giggling when Rolf tried to pull the bed clothes off of her and with a beaming smile on his face when he succeeded.

"Did you truly not hear your hound respond every time you keened my name in the bathtub?" he asked, tracing his finger along her hip.

"Stop teasing me, my lord. I told you I did not."

How embarrassing that her dog had responded loudly to her cries of passion. That passion had only increased after they'd reached their room and the unfettered joys of the bed. The angle of the sunlight indicated that she had slept much later than her usual rising time. Yet who could blame her after the exertions of the night.

The only blight was when she couldn't find the sachet of fertility seeds, which had disappeared from her room, no doubt tidied away by an overzealous servant. Augusta was determined to cement her newfound closeness with Helen, now that they were both married women, by asking her for more. She also wanted to know, if her flow arrived in the weeks to come proving she was not with child, how long she ought to wait to try again for an heir. Or did one do what she and Rolf had done even during one's flow?

Helen and James's room was empty so she headed for Wesley's to see if he knew his sister-in-law's whereabouts. Again, an empty chamber. As she was leaving, one of Wesley's retinue entered, curtsied low to Augusta and stepped back to let her pass. It was then that Augusta noticed her pretty lace cap.

"What is your name?" she asked her.

"Susan, m'lady."

"That cap upon your head. Is it the only one you have?"

"Yes'm." She looked at Augusta curiously.

"I merely wondered because I found one just like it and yet you have yours."

Susan's face cleared with understanding. "We all wear 'em the same in Master Wesley's house. It must be Maura's, as only the two of us came with him."

Augusta felt a shiver of shock. So it was one of *his* servants who had been lurking outside her sitting room on the second floor with no reason to be in that wing of the castle. True, Wesley had arrived right after Perry's injury. However, he and his entourage could have already been in the area.

"I see," she said at last, walking past the girl, her mind in a whirl.

Could the threat truly be Wesley, who always seemed the embodiment of goodness? Yet why had he never married? Perhaps waiting for her to get desperate enough with time running out that she would marry him whether she wanted to or not. Perhaps killing off her suitors but never threatening her because there was no need to do so—until it became apparent that a wedding would occur.

She could start carrying an heir any day. Did that make the danger even greater? If it was Wesley, why had he not slit her throat on the deserted grange the day before?

She was halfway down the stairs when she realized she'd told him that Rolf had walked out on their wedding night. Had that grain of information caused him to spare her life? As long as he thought she and Rolf stayed in separate rooms, the need to kill one of them was not as imperative.

She must talk to Rolf right away. And belatedly, as she reached the bottom of the stairs without being tripped by a furry canine, she wondered, *Where was her hound?*

"CAPTAIN," CAME A FEMALE voice, and he turned to see Helen Brenville hurrying across the courtyard.

He waited for her to catch up, feeling in a better mood than he had since . . . since Trafalgar! And to think, Gus was his today and his tonight, too, and the next day after that.

"I wished to speak with you last night," Helen said, "but you and Augusta disappeared from dinner so quickly, and I didn't see you at the late supper either."

By then, he and Gus had been thoroughly enjoying the joys of matrimony.

"What do you want with me, madam?"

"A small matter, I hope. My husband has a great desire to go to sea. Now that we are related, I wonder if you could gain him a commission. I would be extremely grateful."

He couldn't help offering her a smile. She was so like a mother asking a favor for her child instead of a wife. Was James aware of this request?

"If your husband were to go into his Majesty's navy, you would see little of him for months at a time? It is a better profession for the unmarried bachelor, quite frankly."

"I understand. However, to put a fine point to it, the income would be most welcome."

He frowned. "You live under Wesley's roof by his grace, do you not?"

She nodded. "Quite betwixt the two of us, my lord, my brother-in-law charges us dearly to live with him. Too much, I think. Yet we cannot afford to move out, nor to find a place spacious enough for our growing family. Wesley said he has a notion—a plan, he called it—to help both him and my husband, but as yet, he has not shared it with us."

The plan that jumped to Rolf's mind was marrying a poor heiress and selling her castle. Any number of nobility and even royalty would pay a lot for Thornbury. Alternately, Wesley could move his whole family into the castle and then sell his current holdings. The horrifying truth was that Wesley didn't need to marry Gus. He could inherit Thornbury with or without her as his wife.

"Will you excuse me?" he asked Helen, while he was already backing away.

If anything, their wedding had put Gus in more danger than before. After all, the wedding was only the first hurdle. Wesley might still kill Gus at any time before she begat an heir and the castle would go to him.

Helen called after him, "Indeed, my lord, but the favor?"

What could he say? "Yes, yes, I'll see about a commission." And he was off at a near run to find Gus.

"THERE YOU ARE! I have been searching everywhere . . ." Augusta trailed off when she realized it was not her husband but rather Wesley who was leaning with his head into the stall where Rolf's horse usually resided. If she hadn't wanted so badly to see Rolf, her mind wouldn't have conjured him by mistake, and she would have realized by the cut of her cousin's coat immediately who it was.

"Searching for me?" Wesley asked, offering her his usual smile, that now appeared as a sly false grin.

"No," she said, trying to keep her voice steady. "I was looking for my lord."

"*Your lord.* How odd to hear such words from your mouth, Coz. I can't imagine you addressing me as such had we married."

She started. "Us? Marry? What an idea!" she said, thinking her best course of action was to escape to where there were more people. People who weren't possibly lunatic murderers.

He laughed. "There were a few who thought it a good idea to keep both the Brenville estates in the family."

"Yes," she agreed. "And what do *you* think?" Perhaps he would simply confess.

He tilted his head. "I can see the merit if you and I had wanted to pursue such a path."

"Yet we didn't," she reminded him, thinking he still seemed such an unlikely murderer.

"Have things smoothed over between you and your new husband?"

Why would he ask that? To determine whether the time was ripe to kill her? She simply wouldn't answer. Then she heard one of the grooms walking nearby and felt safer, emboldened enough to speak plainly.

"Wesley, why are you here at this stall?"

"James asked me to meet him and look at your fine horses. You know his penchant for seating himself upon a pretty mount." He shook his head slightly, "However, I haven't seen any particularly remarkable horses except for your husband's and his friend's. And I haven't seen hide nor hair of James."

"Here I am."

Augusta turned. What she saw so plainly confused her that she took a step back. James, a few feet away, had a pistol aimed at her . . . *and* at Wesley.

"What are you doing, James?" Wesley spoke first. "Is this a jest?"

"Get into the stall behind you, with Rolf's horse."

"That's madness. The brute could crush us both," Wesley protested.

"Exactly," James said. "Both of you, or I shoot Augusta now."

He cocked the pistol.

"Stop it," Wesley said, but he started to open the stall. Augusta noted that he did so extremely slowly, giving Rolf's horse a moment to adjust and to back up. Even while following orders, Wesley asked, "Are you insane, brother?"

James merely leveled the pistol at Augusta's chest. "Hurry."

"For what purpose?" Wesley asked, slipping inside the gate and hushing the horse with soothing tones.

"Move quickly, you, too," James said to Augusta.

"I thought you were going to shoot me," she said. "Must I be trampled as well as shot?"

"If you don't go in, I'll shoot you, and Wesley will be blamed."

"Why ever would *I* be blamed?" he asked.

James laughed. "Our cousin's husband is about ready to run you through anyway, dear brother. Hadn't you noticed?"

Augusta edged into the stall with Wesley while Rolf's horse began to rear in fright. Where was Rolf? Whichever of the Rolfs—for either man or hound would be useful at this moment.

"While in there," James stated, "you two will discuss your plans to keep her new husband's money while having an ill-timed hasty tryst."

"Good God," Wesley exclaimed. "You *are* a madman!"

"Unfortunately, your lust for one another will spell your doom, and I will end up with both estates."

Rolf's horse pawed at the ground, bucking its large head, and prancing closer to the invading humans.

"Let them go," Rolf's voice reached Augusta's ears over the threatening sounds of the horse's whinnying.

She watched James whirl around to find Rolf blocking the entrance, holding his service pistol.

"You have been discovered," her husband continued.

"Then you shall have to be shot, as well," James said, barely hesitating though he kept his weapon trained on her. "I have waited too long for Thornbury, worked too hard."

"Did you kill for it?" Augusta asked.

James ignored her, backing up a step and sliding the crossbar to the stall without ever taking his eyes off Rolf. "Drop your gun or I shoot her."

Rolf didn't move, and Augusta was certain she would die in another instant. When the sound of a discharging pistol rang out, she squeezed her eyes closed, awaiting the pain. Nothing.

When she opened them, she saw James sprawled on the stable floor and Perry's smoking gun aimed through the window.

Rolf's horse, even more agitated by the gunshot, struck Wesley's back with his front hoof, sending him careening into her. Putting his arms around her, her cousin attempted to shield her with his body.

Issuing calming words to his charger, Rolf rushed to release the captives, before clanging closed the stall door once more. He took Augusta into his arms, and she let him envelop her with his warmth and strength.

Over her shoulder, he said to Perry, "Impeccable timing, Lieutenant. As usual."

Perry appeared a moment later in the stable doorway, and Augusta watched his steady, somber approach taking in the scene next to the open stall.

"I'm sorry if you had another plan, Captain, but I didn't think you should be the one to kill a member of the Brenville family."

Kill a member of her family. Hearing the words, Augusta's body, already trembling, began to shake out of her control, and suddenly, she was cold all over. Rolf began to briskly rub her back.

"It's finished, now," he murmured against her hair.

"I can't believe it was James," she said, lifting her cheek from his chest. Then she thought of the awful shock to Wesley.

Pushing out of Rolf's arms, she turned to her cousin who was on his knees beside his younger brother.

"He's dead," Wesley said.

"I am very sorry," she told him.

He stood then. "No, I am sorry for what my brother has done, not only to you but to his own family. What am I going to tell his widow?"

Perry had found a horse blanket and carefully draped it over the body. "The widow might be a party to this nastiness," he said, startling Augusta and Wesley both.

"No," she said. "Helen has been the epitome of helpfulness since she arrived."

"You mean by giving you this," Rolf asked.

He held out the sachet to her, and she felt the blood drain from her face. "How did you get that?"

"Millie found it and gave it to Bernadine to ask what the seeds were."

"But they were only to help us," Augusta started to say.

"They will keep your womb barren," Perry chimed in. "That's what Bernadine said."

She looked to Rolf, and he nodded.

"That's when we came to find you, suspecting James was the culprit."

"But Helen is a mother and even now is with child." Augusta couldn't conceive of such wickedness, not in a mother.

"The only one who can tell us with any certainty if she were a part of this scheme is now dead," Wesley observed, his voice weary. "Perhaps she was merely following my brother's orders, or perhaps she didn't even know what the plant really did. He might have told her a lie."

"In any case, I don't want her near Gus again," Rolf said.

"I agree," Wesley said.

Augusta put her hand on her cousin's arm. To her eyes, he looked years older and her heart ached for his loss and the deceit perpetrated upon him.

"I will let her and her children continue to live under my roof," he said. "If she is innocent, it is a kindness I can do. If she is guilty," he shrugged, "still, there is little point in having her hang and leave the children motherless. She has nothing to gain by harming you further, now that the possibility of her taking Thornbury has expired along with her husband.

"I wish it had been otherwise," Augusta said, wanting now to be submerged in a hot bath to chase away the terrible chills still racing through her. Wrapping her arms around herself, all three men held out their coats to her. She stepped toward her husband, and Rolf draped his carefully around her shoulders.

ENSCONCED IN THE HOTTEST water the household could manage, Augusta lay with her head back against the tub, her mind still unable to take in the treachery of the recent events. Beside her, on a stool, Rolf sat, having told her he wouldn't let her out of his sight, at least, not in the foreseeable future. Not until all the guests had left.

And her hound was once more nearby, just outside the door, released from the closet into which someone, most probably James, had secured him with the lure of a juicy bone.

She had started to tell Rolf how she'd ended up in the stables and then had lapsed into silence, now realizing that she was whistling, quietly but steadily. Abruptly, she stopped, opened her eyes, and looked into the intelligent gaze of her husband.

"I went indoors to find you and came across Millie in a terrible state. She'd found the seeds in your room—"

"Helen said they would increase my fertility," she told him. "It wasn't that I doubted your abilities, my lord."

"Doubted my . . .? I don't understand."

"The seeds, Helen said, were also supposed to bolster the power of your . . . *um* . . . your . . ." Her cheeks reddened.

He raised his eyebrows. "I quite understand, but that is *not* what the plant does."

"It's not poisonous, is it?"

His face clouded over. "Not exactly, except to your womb. The seeds stop life growing there."

She raised a hand to her mouth. "Sweet Mary, don't let that be true."

"It is. Bernadine was well familiar with it. Queen Anne's Lace, she called it. Apparently, women take it with great success in certain situations."

Like Millie's, Augusta suddenly realized. How else could her maid lie with Jared and not conceive? "Then we are doomed."

"No, Gus. It is temporary, thus the need to keep ingesting the plant."

She closed her eyes and breathed out, relief washing over her. She had not stupidly lost her birthright by trusting Helen.

"Bernadine has been extremely valuable, has she not?" she asked, her eyes still closed.

"Perry certainly holds her in the highest esteem," Rolf remarked.

Augusta blinked back at him. Maybe there would be another wedding in the not-too-distant future. Then she realized an awful implication.

"Helen cannot possibly have eaten those seeds and conceived three babes, could she?"

"No." He stared at her as she accepted the truth.

"Then she truly was guilty of trying to stop us from creating an heir. And in all likelihood, she poisoned my wine."

"Or her maid did. One of her servants came along with Wesley."

"Maura," she murmured.

"How did you know?" he asked.

"The cap we found was hers. I was coming to tell you when I encountered Wesley. I thought the servant worked for him, and then . . . James arrived." Augusta groaned. "Helen is a mother? How could she do this?"

He was silent.

Then she sat up abruptly as a notion struck her, unmindful of the water dripping off her breasts until she heard him take in a quick breath and saw where his gaze had landed. She crossed her arms over her chest. "I just thought of something."

"I am thinking of something, too," he said, leaning down to kiss her.

The feel of his lips on hers chased away much of the lingering fear that had hung over her head like a stubborn rain cloud. His tongue slipped into her mouth and for a moment, all thoughts seemed to drain from her head.

Against her mouth, he murmured, "Come out of the bath, now, Gus, and let me love you."

"Love me?" she spluttered, leaning away from him.

"Yes, dear wife, for I do—very much—love you."

"How astounding! For I, too, have found that you are quite in my heart. I love you, dear husband."

He took her hand, and she stood up and let him wrap a drying cloth around her and begin to rub her dry.

"Come to bed," he said, with a smile. "That's an order, and you are going to be an obedient wife, yes? At least, sometimes."

"That's what I was about to say when you kissed me," she remembered. "Whatever else she did, Helen did not shoot the arrow at Perry, nor kill my suitors. That must have been James or someone in his employ. So perhaps she was merely being an obedient wife when she gave me the Queen Anne's Lace."

"Your point?" he asked, helping her into her robe so they could escape the bathing room for their bedroom. Then he placed in her hands the mug of spiced wine that Millie had insisted she drink to soothe her.

"Obedience can be dangerous," she pointed out.

"Well, we'll compromise, then. I will seek your counsel on all things to do with the castle."

She gasped at his unexpected words.

"And," he continued, "you will be obedient when it doesn't seem dangerous for you to be so."

He was teasing her, but she didn't mind for her new husband loved her! Moreover, she knew he would, indeed, take her advice on running their home.

"I will ever be grateful that of all the men in England, you were the one who betrothed yourself to me," she told him, feeling a tad shy about her declaration.

He gave her a glimpse of his sensuous grin with the piratical gap between his teeth, and she dropped her mug upon his foot. Both bending to retrieve it, they knocked heads.

"Oh dear," she said, but Rolf only laughed.

"Promise me, Lady Gus, that you won't try to change yourself, not your hair," he said pointedly, "nor your mannerisms, nor ever cease your infernal whistling, for you are quite perfect, precisely as you are."

She nodded, feeling herself infused with warmth that was not due to the bathwater.

They left the chamber, carefully stepping over Rolf and letting the sleeping dog lie.

ALSO BY SYDNEY JANE BAILY

BEASTLY LORDS
Lord Despair
Lord Anguish
Lord Vile
Lord Darkness
Lord Misery
Lord Wrath
Lord Corsair
Eleanor

RAKES ON THE RUN
Last Dance in London
Pursued in Paris
Banished to Brighton
Gretna Green by Sunset

DIAMONDS OF THE FIRST WATER
Clarity
Purity
Adam
Radiance
Brilliance

RARE CONFECTIONERY
The Duchess of Chocolate
The Toffee Heiress
My Lady Marzipan

DEFIANT HEARTS
An Improper Situation
An Irresistible Temptation
An Inescapable Attraction
An Inconceivable Deception
An Intriguing Proposition
An Impassioned Redemption

ABOUT THE AUTHOR

USA Today bestselling author Sydney Jane Baily writes historical romance, set in Victorian England, late 19th-century America, the Middle Ages, the Georgian era, and the Regency period. She believes in happily-ever-after stories with engaging characters and attention to period detail.

Born and raised in California, she has traveled the world, spending an inordinate amount of time in the U.K. where her extended family resides. She loves eating fish and chips, drinking shandy, and snacking on Maltesers and Cadbury bars.

After obtaining degrees in English literature and in history, besides writing novels, she has spent time as a copyeditor, cat snuggler, website designer, production editor, mother of two, and faithful friend to her dog, among other endeavors both literary and not.

Sydney currently lives in New England with her family—human, canine, and feline. You can learn more about her books, read her blog, and contact her via her website at SydneyJaneBaily.com.